Golly Gee

and the Smidgens

A Family Reunited

R. Evans Pansing

Order this book online at www.trafford.com
or email orders@trafford.com

Most Trafford titles are also available at major online book retailers.

Printed in Victoria, BC, Canada.

ISBN: 978-1-4269-2409-5 (sc)

Library of Congress Control Number: 2009913220

*Our mission is to efficiently provide the world's finest, most comprehensive
book publishing service, enabling every author to experience success.
To find out how to publish your book, your way, and have it available
worldwide, visit us online at www.trafford.com*

Trafford rev. 11/30/2009

 www.trafford.com

North America & international
toll-free: 1 888 232 4444 (USA & Canada)
phone: 250 383 6864 ♦ fax: 812 355 4082

Thanks to wife and uncle Darrel
and Jim Hansel for encouragement

Golly Gee- Mansion manager

Mr. Snooty- Real Estate broker

Bakka Beans – Mansion cook and chef

Flinch Pinching- possible Mansion buyer

Redd Peppers- Chauffer and handyman

Penelope Pinching- Wife of Flinch

Empire Uppity- master of Rustic realm

Swoop- Fussy's giant flying moth

Mater Uppity- Wife of Empire

Glide- Fidget's giant flying moth

Jump- Adoptive son of Uppity's

Nibbles- Fussy's riding house mouse

Fidget- Smidgen boy

Twitch- Fidget's riding house mouse

Fussy Smidgen girl

Bark Gruffly- Jump's kidnaper

Graybub- Smidgen Elder

Nastine Gruffly- Wife of Bark

Oldene- wife of Graybub

Crinkle-another Smidgen Elder

Peyton- mansion cat

"The Bright Ones"=Fidget & Fussy

Prologue

ustic realm was a great mansion far out of town where Mr. and Mrs. Uppity lived. Mr. Empire Uppity was a successful factory owner and Mrs. Mater Uppity was a wonderful housewife and host to many charitable events and ministries. Having no children they adopted a young boy, named Jump. In the recent past Jump was kidnapped and never found by the police or FBI.

Jump had raced to the far away road to meet the school bus, not heeding his mother's caution to wait for her. When she finally arrived at the road, she was not able to locate her adopted son. She called, and called, and then waited until the school bus came. Her worst fears came crashing down around her after talking to the bus driver who mentioned he had not picked up the boy but that someone else could have taken the boy into school. She knew Jump would not go with any stranger, as he was a very shy boy. Returning to her mansion, she called the school to see if Jump had arrived by any means. The answer being "no" a great lump raised up in her throat as kidnapping became a logical answer. Mater called Mr. Uppity and he in returned alerted the police who brought in the FBI. The officials questioned every body even remotely connected to the young boy. A search was made along the bus route and around the school. After several weeks, the inquiries began to diminish, as a ransom phone call with an exorbitant ransom from Strangeville. That was where the authorities concentrated their search. The search around the mansion was casual at best. Because the kidnapping occurred at the road and the ransom call was from Strangeville.

This kidnapping left the mansion and its occupants in limbo. Sadness pervades the entire mansion and its occupants. The mansion was purchased with the young boy in mind. A young boy of seven was the apple of their eyes and to all of Rustic Realm's inhabitants, including the diminutive Smidgens that loved Jump.

Golly Gee was the lady manager of the entire mansion's operations. Her two close associates, Bakka Beans, the cook and Redd Peppers, the chauffer were the only ones that also knew about the existence of the Smidgens. The Smidgens were little people that lived in the mansion unknown to all other employees and even the owners. These Smidgens were about the size of a fat man's thumb, but very animated and normal in other respects. The owners of the mansion were Mr. Empire Uppity and his wife Mrs. Mater Uppity

The Smidgens moved into the house after several terrible killer winters that just about wiped out the Smidgen genre. The Smidgens became susceptible to the diminishing shelter habitat and increased chemical pesticides being used on the outside. The cat, Peyton, was also a threat outside where he manifested natural tendencies of the hunter, killer type, but was manageable on the inside of the mansion.

Smidgens being small people of the legendary type, the larger world about them presented many new challenges on the inside. Places to hid and people to avoid where among the challenges. Fussy, a girl, and Fidget, a boy, are the two young Smidgens that move about the mansion still trying to plan a way to investigative where and if the young boy jump might yet be found. One way would be a flight in the high atmosphere to observe areas overlooked by the local officials giving them new hope that Jump could be found. Their young eyes could see things that others might miss.

After much cajoling, Golly Gee gave her permission for Fidget and Fussy oft times, Called the Bright Ones, to mount their giant moths for a high flying ride to see as much of the mansions' grounds as possible and in the distant woods and glens. These two are the only one's that dared ride the moths so high in the air. The temerity of the other Smidgens was the Bright Ones' chance to do many feats of daring.

The flight was being arranged on the same day that the Uppitys were away, and the spring-cleaning was in full force. The mansion is a beehive of activity so that the flight is not easily noticed or forbidden by the elders.

CHAPTER
ONE

*T*he sounds and excitement that came through the mansion at Rustic Realm were boisterous but welcome. Doors and windows were being opened and shut in quick succession. The activity level indicator must be close to the top of the scale. The spring air was exhilarating as it began to circulate through the great house like a fairy tale giant heaving and breathing. How little did the grand home know that arcane dark clouds and deceptive forces were moving in its direction? People with spurious intents were about to enter the picture.

Voices floated up to the second floor in a higher pitch and faster pace than usual. The first week of spring was always set aside for this annual house cleaning.

Golly Gee was in charge of a small staff and the center of all the action. Included in the staff was Mr. Brown, the gardener and handyman, Mrs. Main, the maid, Bakka Beans the cook, and Redd Peppers, the chauffeur. Stan the night security guard and Opal the extra day maid made up the very competent staff for Golly to supervise. She was always busy and capable of doing two or three things at once. She moved about the mansion with her intelligent face, permanent smile, and electric personality.

Golly looked much the same, morning or night. All business. Walking the fine line between being in control and yet submissive to a higher authority. Her motions and movements were precise and always had a purpose and resolve.

As Golly entered the North Wing, she was heard walking from a long distance away because of the crispness of her uniforms, and the cadence of her shoes. It was always like this. She was short by modern standards but many found that they looked up to her. Her clean, shiny auburn hair was a perfect-coiled chignon on her head. Neat! Clean! Sharp! Her eyes were bright and sparkled with their piercing indigo regard. Her mouth was soft, with a touch of crimson on her lips, always appearing as a charming smile.

She moved past various rooms on her many errands, quickly glancing into them for reference. 'What a busy day this will be,' she thought as she took an extra deep breath to fuel her movements on this beautiful spring morning.

She seemed to know everything worth knowing. The staff asked many questions about the future of Rustic Realm, and its future inhabitants. Golly Gee had formulated some answers that were informative and applicable." Everything is going to be all right," was her final comment in these discussions. In the days before this special flight, Golly Gee had alerted the Smidgens of the exact day and hour that springhouse cleaning would begin.

Earlier, the Smidgens finished the packing of winter clothes and paraphernalia and accomplished the many tasks that were called for them to move from their winter quarters inside to more spacious summer quarters, outside in the stumps, trees and caves.

Inside quarters was in the upstairs bedrooms of Mr. and Mrs. Uppity, which many Smidgens had the advantage of living in warm clothing all winter. Mr. Uppity had those fine wool jackets; flannel shirts and suits made from the warmest of materials. The Uppitys chose to sleep downstairs after the kidnapping to be closer to any possible news of the boys return.

The two young Smidgens who were almost inseparable great friends (Fidget and Fussy, called the 'Bright Ones by many) lived with their families in some of Mr. Uppity's wool tweed jackets, waiting for spring and probably a return to the outdoors. The clothes were extra apparel not needed by the Uppitys this last winter.

Fidget the boy, was smart as a paper cut. Fast as a boardinghouse, grab, at mealtime. Small in stature by big folks standards but almost full-grown by Smidgen standards. He had a fine looking head that was topped-off by very dark hair that reflected red when the light periodically flashed upon it. His wide, wise, eyes were a deep cobalt blue, and he had ears that were like all Smidgens, prominent. His mouth was even but a little on the firm side. He liked to talk but knew that he had to keep his lips zipped up, or he would never learn anything. A real task. The boy possessed rosy cheeks that sometimes others made fun about. So what! They were only rosy cheeks when exhilarated. A fine boy was Fidget.

Fussy was a young, vibrant, vivacious dynamo of a girl. She is nearly full-grown and is a classical feminine force. Long, dark flowing hair that was similar to polished American Walnut. She was always brushing her hair back behind her excellent ears with a quick flip of her hand. Fidget called it the "Fussy Flick.". Her vivid eyes were an emerald green and projected intensity and intelligence. Her features were petite and yet fully formed and balanced. A mouth that laughed, pouted, smiled, and instructed, all at one time or one at a time. A delight to watch.

On the coldest of winter nights, many Smidgens sought out some of Mrs. Uppity's extra fur coats or jackets. After all, everybody would be there. Fidget and Fussy, however, expressing their independence, sought out the jackets and the long silk lined sleeves of one of the wool tweed's of Mr. Uppity. What fun to slide down those sleeves on a cold winter's day and then to the floor where a fur-lined hat would gently receive them.

From there it was only a hop, skip and a jump to a petite table where all would enjoy some of those tiny marshmallows floating on some hot cocoa that Bakka Beans had prepared in her kitchen.

Those days now behind them for this year, it was time to move on. The new locations would give the Smidgens more opportunity in the warm months to move around and enjoy more of their outdoor spaces without being threatened by any dangerous elements. Birds, cats, severe weather, and even some humans were always a threat to Smidgens that were so small and indefensible.

Some of the Smidgens had used the friendly mice that lived upstairs to move them and their belongings to some of the other rooms and closets in the fall. Mice Muffles and Meeky were Fidget and Fussy's favorite mice to ride. This year Fidget and Fussy were especially anticipating the move. They had a great wish to fly the great Moths before going to their new location. To see what they could see.

They had been granted special permission by Golly Gee to fly the giant tame moths outdoors, as requested. (After all, Golly remained their custodian and self-appointed guardian since they moved into the house.)

They originally planned to fly down to the garden area and around the yard for a pleasant spring flight to check out the woods and lawns. They knew as the moths moved high in the air, before the grand glide down near the flowers and bushes, they would be able to see all the area in the distance they had never really seen before as the older Smidgens had. They knew they would see places no one else had ever seen in years past.

Some of the Smidgen elders had on occasion described some of the features of the land to the Bright Ones. No one had recently expressed a wish to fly up that high to see in all the directions except the inquisitive Fussy and Fidget. Smidgens were not natural born fliers. It was a scary thought to most of them.

Golly had carefully chosen this spring-cleaning day with this event in mind. It must be a clear and warm day to be able to have the moths carry the two Smidgens high up in the air, for their peek at the valley and glen, all the way to the remote dense forest above the fields, consequently, satisfying their investigative natures.

Earlier in the month when there were rainy or windy days, it would have been disastrous and unfruitful. Now, was a day that the Uppitys vacated the premises for some shopping and meetings in the morning concerning the sale of the Rustic Realm, so that there would be no chance for them to witness the high flying inquisitors?

The time was nigh. It was THE cleaning day but Golly still made time for her special people. She thought of them continually as she hurried to find the Bright Ones. She was certain of all the proper conditions had been met. To be sure of the Bright ones timeliness, she searched out the usual closets and hiding places for Fidget and Fussy so that they could begin immediately.

When she found them on the third floor, they were already packed up and ready to go. Each had their own daypack filled with things that might be used on the flight. A pair of tiny binoculars, flight jackets, head cap, water bottle, and even a little snack. A few personal belongings such as string, facial tissue, needle, thread, and gum was in little saddlebags and notes of encouragements that Golly had sewn for them, earlier. Even Redd and Bakka had sent along an item or two that we would see later. The saddlebags would go over the backs of the great moths similar to a mighty steed.

Early in the morning was best, she told them because of the uplifting air currents. The third floor solarium window was opened wide for an easy exit in the crisp morning air. The other Smidgens were not present as they all thought the flight was foolish as well as dangerous, besides being too early in the morning for most of the sleepy heads.

Golly had counseled them last week that Swoop and Glide, good highflying moths and well trained, would be the best companions for this special flight.

The bright Ones already knew this, but in consideration of Golly's love and preparations did not mention it.

She glowed with approval when she saw that they had already heeded all of her advice. Caution and encouragement were expertly woven into her conversations with physician-like skill.

"You both must be careful and obey all of the things I have said about this flight." It was difficult to determine if the Bright Ones minds as well as their elegant ears were tuned-in as they busied their hands and concentrated with the last minute tasks of preparation.

Each saddle was made from one of Mr. Uppitys old belts and the cinches were made from leather shoelaces. Improvisations were what Smidgens were good at doing.

Fidget had his moth that he had trained most of the winter, saddled up first and was raring to go, rosy cheeks, and all. Fussy was confirming, with the help of Golly Gee that all was done to perfection. The cinch was drawn up tight but not so tight that Glide would feel it bite as they flew upon the waves of air and dove down to see the garden. Fussy had seen it all in her dreams last night.

Fussy chimed in with her questions "Is the window open? Are the Uppitys gone? Don't worry about us," all in rapid fire order, as was her energetic nature.

Fidget tried to say something while attempting to wiggle free from Golly Gee with her last minute instructions and her giant kiss. "Oh! Golly, you didn't have to do that. Let's go."

Fussy was still patting her moth Glide and telling Fidget to settle down or Swoop, a finely trained giant moth would take off so fast that Fidget would only being sitting on air. Swoop was always ready for action just like Fidget.

"Do not rub off any of the natural powder-like covering on the moth's wings or take off their daytime flying goggles that I had carefully placed," Golly Gee warned them all sternly as the foursome set to fly as they headed out the opened window. "Be careful."

Off the two went with barely a look back at the waving of Golly gee.

The two Bright Ones had more energy and enthusiasm on their way to an adventure than some others have in a lifetime, thought Golly Gee as she prepared to return to the other Smidgens and her moving chores. The air was as soft and warm as one of Mr. Uppity's great winter gloves. Fidget and Fussy flew out the window of the upstairs solarium, effortlessly. Swoop the moth, with Fidget on board was in the lead as usual. Glide was close by with Fussy holding on tightly to the reins. The two powerful moths, with protective eye goggles, began to climb into the spring morning air with the greatest of ease.

After some tasks in another part of the mansion, Golly found herself back on the third floor. She was drawn to the open solarium window, looking for any signs of the fearless foursome. She trusted them all and yet still had to know where they were and how they were doing. It was a motherly thing.

She rather casually looked at first, telling herself not

to be too intense, but when only the usual spring sights were seen, Golly began to squint and search the air with more diligence.

Just below, she saw the gardens and bushes. Some were just beginning to show signs of life. Buds ready to pop out and blossom into beautiful flowers or leaves.

She could see that the gardener was busy with all the spring activities getting the gardens into tiptop shape. Mr.Brown was the mansion's gardener. He pruned and fertilized as well as mulched all around the plants to keep them in a healthy and attractive condition. He was an elderly gentleman with stooped shoulders and twinkling blur eyes. His hands were callused but his heart was soft as was his voice. He had a green thumb if ever there was one.

Seeing no Fidget and no Fussy, Golly Gee pulled out her glasses and put them on, hoping that would help. She had told them not to go too far and not to stay out of range too long. Her only thought was a kindly, "Kids!"

"Take your time and be careful," her own words echoed in her mind. There was danger out there that none of the foursome had ever been exposed to. All Golly Gee's advice was given with much love, and it pleased her that they had, up to now, paid attention to her warnings.

Only time would tell whether an inch of caution is worth a mile of remedy. She told them that you don't have to be bitten by a shark to know it has sharp teeth.

Faith to trust these loved ones came with some difficulty because they were always impetuous and bold. Others in the Smidgen clan often teased the two, because they failed in some of their unconventional endeavors.

They tried many things and received many bruises and BAND-AIDS for their rewards.

Golly's heart ached for the Bright Ones, knowing the agony and pain of growing up with those qualities.

Out of the corner of her eye, she saw some movement and focused in that direction with all her attention. She drew in her breath with a little gasp as she saw several large and threatening bumblebees gathering and hanging around an area in the gardens down below. The bumbles were way too close to the Smidgens' flight area.

Golly Gee, knowing the danger those bumbles presented, hurried down from the third floor solarium. Down the hall and using the back stairs, she moved down with urgency to the ground floor. Eventually, she would get a better view and be in a position to help the two little Smidgens if they needed it. If she could get down to the back yard in time, she could help, she thought as she neared the kitchen door. Danger should never alter friendships.

Several of the staff tried to ask questions as Golly sailed down to the back door. "What is the matter?" Blurted Mrs. Main the maid, picking up her mop to allow Golly free access. Even Bakka Beans tried to evoke some comments from Golly.

What's happening? Where are you going? Can I help any?"

She gave no heed to their voices. She had one thing on her mind at this moment. "Only she and her fly swatter could help," she uttered through clenched lips.

CHAPTER
TWO

*F*idget had talked earlier with Fussy about the high flight. "We need to deviate from Golly's plan just a little to see where no one had looked before. I know we can make a difference concerning Jump's disappearance. Let's get as high as we can so we can observe all of the great fields and woods that others have not searched with any diligence." Although it might be a little risky, both had agreed to chance the first few precious moments to rise as high as they could, thereby enabling them to see as far as possible.

With the wind rushing through their hair, casting glints of polished walnut and flecks of deep red as the morning sun began its daily revolution. The two Smidgens soon saw the top of the mansion pass beneath them. Holding fast the reins until their knuckles turned white, the two little pilots now were in a cooler stratum of air.

The ride was so spectacular that it gave them each the shivers for a few seconds. The air was full of all the smells one would expect outside on a spring morning. The outdoor aromas of spring seemed to power the moth's energies and abilities. The Lilacs were sending their sweet perfume up and into the nostrils of the little adventurers. Mingled with the smell of newly cut grass and freshly plowed earth, the aromas were heady. They could see that far below, some bumblebees were milling about the flowers at the corner of the great mansion.

It was the nature of bumbles to fly high and harass any other flyers in their space. With that in mind, the bumbles began to move up in the air towards the Smidgens with nothing good in mind. Their advancement was not welcomed. The bumbles distantly posed no threat. A slight, evasive maneuver was in order by the Smidgens pulling the moths miniscule bridles, just before the bumbles were no longer in sight.

The Bright Ones finally moved above the treetops with only a few beads of perspiration on their foreheads. They had finally attained a magnificent elevation to view all the country surroundings. Trees in full leaf, berry bushes in bloom, a babbling brook coming down through the lands, a small pond with emerging cattails, fruit trees sporting an array of blossoms and all mulched around to a perfection that only Mr. brown was responsible.

That was not enough for the young twosome. Higher and higher, they encouraged their powdery mounts to go. Each Smidgen trying their mounts to out-do the other's. The results were equal and exhilarating.

Far out in front of them was a cold flowing stream with its own alluring valley. It was like an enchanted glen with gentle banks on each side. Shortly, the stream and the glen turned into a deep wood and disappeared. The woods marched up to the right to some plowed fields that had been recently planted. Straight ahead, the forest advanced up a hill and finally thinned out at the top of the little hill. Before the forest thinned out, they both noticed something nestled deep among woodlands thick foliage. It appeared to be a small blue-green- house with a brown roof, looking much like its surroundings. Very small, maybe one or two rooms. That abode was more like a cabin than a house. This was not supposed to be. This was the Uppity's property and no dwelling was ever allowed in the woods. If what they saw was real, it was out of place and an anomaly on the landscape.

It barely came into view as the two Bright Ones reached the top of their flight. A quick glance was all that was seen as the moths circled at their maximum height. Each flight around called for a turn of their heads and readjustments for focusing. The house was situated in a place that appeared to have no lane or driveway. Although far off, you could tell that the house was plain and had a roof that was similar to camouflage. A little finger of smoke came from its tiny chimney.

The mounts began to fatigue due to the long ascent. In the higher layers of air, the moths were buffeted by the winds and without much coaxing, circled several times in a coasting fashion that rested them before the long, slow ride back down to friendlier and calmer conditions.

Riding the thermals was an adventure in itself. Wave after wave of warm air gave them a roller coaster ride as they circled and swooped returning to just above the Rustic Realm area. Breathless and giddy with joy, Fidget and Fussy finally steered Glide and Swoop to descend to a pleasant area in the grape arbor.

The Smidgens are tiny people that often rode the giant moths for fun and investigations. They can't fly with out riding on the backs of the giant moths.

After a long and enjoyable descent, they glided into the grape arbor area and headed for the high wooden beams that made an excellent, safe landing strip. Their hands almost numb from holding on tight, the two little travelers dismounted their moths rather gingerly and slowly unpacked their refreshments. Bakka Beans had earlier prepared for a little picnic lunch they had packed in the saddlebags.

The moths rolled their eyes towards some flowers in the area, and the Smidgens knew they had to eat also. The Moths received the signal, thumbs up and hand pointing to some near-by flowers for permission to go off and feed for a while.

Fidget and Fussy had time to rest and just hang out. The picnic was superb. Cheese, crackers, and little sandwiches along with celery sticks, small carrots with Bakka's special dip completed this little picnic.

The Moths had flown off with their long tongues ready to extract nectar from some of the local flowers.

Fussy wiped her mouth with a tiny napkin and rolled herself up in a nearby leaf after a Fussy Flick, (her flip of her head to reposition her long and lovely hair,) and then fashioning an old spider web as a pillow.

Fidget nestled up in an old deserted bird's nest, after some preliminary squirming, began to close his eyes for a quick nap. Before dozing off, he just happened to look down below his safe haven. To his surprise, he spied Peyton, the cat, checking out the tall grasses. It was surely, by chance, that the sighting of the cat was made.

Peyton the cat was large and sable from nose tip to tail thereby blending into shadows. The tip of the tail was the only part that was not jet-black. His Benevolent Maker created the cat's tail tip pure white. Waving that small, pure white tip, held high in his pounce mode had been the only signal that gave proof that Peyton was in the vicinity or even alive. He would sit or lay perfectly still for long periods of time not moving a muscle. Upon close examination, a serious observer would note that the tail tip was moving ever so slightly, like a miniature white gloved hand. It was Peyton's bit of imperfection in his hunting style.

It was moving now as he concentrated on some high grass that might contain a little bird or even an unsuspecting vole. His eyes were orange with a black perpendicular slit that became larger when close to the pounce time.

None of these characteristics seemed to be present when Peyton was in the house with one of the Uppitys in residence and in close proximity. There, he appeared to be the perfect, helpless little pussycat. Indoors, he appears as a cute, cuddly, furry kitty. There, he only exposes little padded rounded paws. Here, in the great outdoors they are artistically crafted claws of terror. A paradox in behavior, thought Fidget.

Here, far from the house and in his natural element, Peyton tightly evolves into a ball of fur that he unconsciously twitches his tail to signal his presence. A dynamo that appeared is a threat to all small beings.

Fidget observed the suspected feline menace far below

the grape arbor with the caution that had been instilled into him by his guardians and teachers. No noise. No sudden movements. No telling activity. It would be best to wait, thought Fidget. Even to awake Fussy would be a risk. He hoped that the cat would eventually leave. It was important that the Bright Ones went unnoticed. After all, Peyton could climb wooden posts and they couldn't.

After some time Fussy, began to wiggle and yawn.

"Be quiet," whispered Fidget to his awakening friend, as he pointed down below, carefully with one finger. Fussy moved with a slow and careful motion as she rolled over to look beyond the great wooden beam in the arbor and down to the possible danger. Black and unmoving except for a little white flag on the end of his tail,

Peyton waited. There was movement in the grass, and Peyton immediately pounced with explosive energy in a specific direction in the tall grass. There was a scramble and growling by Peyton, as the unseen victim must be making lightning quick evasive movements. A few hisses, and then Peyton seemed to be puzzled as he turned in circles on his tiptoes. Peyton's arched back surrendered with a heave and a final defeated little hiss ended the hunt. The intended target had escaped the shrewd and cunning black cat. The little vole had outwitted the cat by natural cunning in the grass.

All this was not very important, thought Fidget, as both Bright Ones sighed a big relief. That big bold black tabby gets plenty of opportunities for all kinds of food in the big mansion. He is given fancy food out of cans and plenty of goodies that Bakka Beans, offers the house pet every day. This event just witnessed is just pure and simple instinct harking back to the cat family's origins.

This exercise was for the art of his craft, thought Fidget. Slowly and with calculated care the whiskered Peyton began to stroll off towards the house.

At this point, the two Smidgens would like to see the missing moths and order their return. Fussy picked up her binoculars and began to make a sweep of the flowers in the distance.

The two separated moths were causally flying around some of the most brilliant flowers at Rustic Realm. The mansion and surrounding grounds had been tendered and cared for by Mr. Brown for many years. 'Plantings for beauty,' was Mr. Brown's slogan. The flowers and bushes all had been planted with that attractiveness in mind.

Fussy then used her shiny mirror to make flashes in that direction to get their attention to return. The two moths immediately began the return to the top of the grape arbor.

The moth's rise was slow because their tummies were full, and the sun was high and warm. After landing, Swoop and Glide rolled their eyes to show a need to sleep.

"Oh, no, you don't," said Fussy. "We are ready to return to the mansion." She snapped. In a very short time, the picnic things were repacked and all was made ready to fly again.

"Saddle up," barked Fidget as he checked the cinch and swung up on the back of Swoop. Fussy did the same to Glide. She also verified her mount had retracted its tongue from nectar feeding and had wide-awake eyes for the trip back. Fussy gave a "Fussy flick" and was ready.

With a little push up, the two winged wonders

headed into the wind and began a slow climb. A slight tug on the reins pulled their mounts around to head for the house. A slow glide down to the open window of the third floor solarium was the final phase of an exciting spring day.

CHAPTER
THREE

The sun was beginning to set in the late afternoon, filling the sky with pink clouds and orange swirls. No one was at the window or even in the room as the riders flew in and prepared to land. They landed in the third floor solarium as planned. Once there, they would gain their bearings and know what was going on in the mansion.

There was a special place for Bakka to grow herbs for her savory cooking delights. The room always seems to be especially cheerful, summer, or winter. That is probably why the Uppitys hardly ever came here. Cheerfulness was something the Uppitys found difficult to experience any more.

Fidget and Fussy brought more cheer into the room as they cruised the length of the area and landed on the back of a large plush glider in the one end of the room.

A glider, being a sofa size settee that rocks or glides when sitting on its comfy cushions. When the saddles, goggles, and reins were off, the two moths crawled to the back of the glider's pad, out of sight, and proceeded to go to sleep. Fidget and Fussy carefully looked around to be certain they landed unnoticed by the mansion's tabby before calling for the two mice that they would rely on for transportation in the house. The two trained mice the Bright Ones rode when in the house could be called for if near by if convenient for the mice.

This was a change in their plans but considering all that the moths had done up to now it seemed sensible to use the mice for their final leg of their adventure and to return to their families.

The moths were full of food and tired. The Bright Ones were full of sights and excitement. Carefully Fidget called out for their mice, Nibbles and Twitch, before they would hazard a trip to the floor to make their next move. No answer. It was time to make a thoughtful decision as they huddled together to discuss their choices.

They waited a long time after hearing the Uppitys returning in the family sports utility vehicle as Golly had inferred earlier in the day. They continued to wait patiently for the mice to appear before they would venture farther into the house. 'It is difficult to wait so much," said Fussy with a face that was not very pretty.

"I think old people are just slower and as are mice and moths. We have so much to do where as the others are just hanging around waiting for young people to make plans," Fidget added to her thought.

All seemed rather still except for the hum of the Big Cadillac outside. It must be leaving the garage with important dignitaries wanting to buy Rustic Realm. They were going out to the main road because the sound was fading to the West. The Caddy was used when Mr. and Mrs. Uppity wanted to transport guests. It was used when bringing them in or taking them back to the big City. Evidently, Redd Peppers was returning some renowned persons back to the city.

CHAPTER

FOUR

*G*olly Gee ran into the kitchen and found Bakka Beans bustling as usual with her pots and pans. Even though breakfast was over, the sweet aroma of hot cakes and crisp bacon was still heavy in the air. The kitchen was very large and contained all the necessary equipment for making many tasty meals for many hungry appetites.

In the center of the room was a large butcher-block table with great pots and pans hanging above it. Cauldrons to whisks, pots and pans a wok here and an iron skillet there were both functional and decorative.

A black wood-burning stove was in evidence. Bakka was of the old school when wood-burning stoves added to the flavor of her foods. Out of this imposing, mammoth, iron works came the most delicious of foods and culinary concoctions man or Smidgen has ever known.

Golly gave Bakka a quick salutation and asked for a large towel and a fly swatter to scare away the annoying bumble bees that were flying menacingly outside the kitchen door, around the back of the house. Bakka could see the intensity of Golly's errand and swiftly handed to Golly a fly swatter and towel to do the job. Bakka gave a quick encouraging word to the fast moving Golly, "go get them, Golly! If I can help just give me a call."

Just as quickly, Golly was through the door and outside, glancing at the flowered bushes that she had originally seen those annoying, Bumble Bees. She was so concerned that they might spot the two flying moths and attempt to harass them and their two tiny passengers.

Golly saw the bumbles and gave a wave of the towel while wielding the swatter complete with a loud "shoo!" They flew off in response to Golly Gee's efforts, flying higher than her reach. They turned the corner of the house where it would be more difficult for Golly to follow. Golly Gee, feeling satisfied that she had finished her mission, again scanned the skies to locate the little travelers. Even with her eyes shaded by her hand she was unable to see any sign of them. She determined in her mind that somehow her act of protection was promising for the little Smidgens.

With a big sigh of relief and resignation, she proceeded to return to the house and to her springhouse cleaning duties.

She returned through the kitchen door and then remembered to tell Bakka to be sure to feed Peyton, the cat, and this morning.

"It would be prudent to feed the cat so that his

appetite would not require him to stalk any little creatures roaming around the lawn and grape arbor."

Bakka confidently replied that she had already prepared a large bowl of food and placed it in its usual place as she always did. If Peyton even got a little hungry, it could be very dangerous for the Smidgen population of the house. "You know I keep that tabby supplied with vittles so his appetite is always satisfied to the advantage of mice and Smidgens." Each smiled knowingly at the other as they passed in the kitchen, continuing to the assignments that the morning had been required of them today.

Golly spun out of the kitchen giving orders left and right to ears that were present and not present. Helpers had been hired to hasten the work. The house had to be cleaned from top to bottom today for the Uppitys had a real estate agent coming later this afternoon to talk over the details of the pending sale of Rustic Realm.

After delegating all the chores again and determining their progress, Golly departed to the garages. She wanted to see how Redd Peppers was progressing to the needs of the many cars he was entrusted to maintain. Changing oil and filters as well as spark plugs seemed to on his agenda very regularly. He also attended to the many auto repairs that the estate called for occasionally. He loved his tools and shop.

She needed to talk to him about the agenda that the Uppity's had given her to establish all times of various activities. She entered the great garage through a little door that had been constructed in one of the roll up electric garage doors from the outside and stepped into another world. The air was heavy with the smell of oil and lubricants.

The concrete floor was clean and shiny from the years of scrubbing it to spotless perfection. Assorted machines, punch press, electric welder, air pump tire changer, battery charger were just some of the equipment that filled every nook and cranny, ready to come alive and perform their assigned function in solving some complex job to keep the Uppity fleet in top running order. A variety of pulleys and coiled apparatus were suspended from the ceiling, having the appearance of the innards of a great creature. A large octagonal clock hung over the far door. Drums for oil and floor creepers to maneuver under the machines while on one's back were to be seen along with an array of containers on shelving were all at attention, waiting to be put into service by their commander.

The place appeared to be filled with automotive objects, and yet there was always a little echo when people spoke within its walls the garage being so large. The cars were all lined up in a row so that they looked like an automobile football team lineup ready to do battle. Shoulder to shoulder and nose to a line that Redd Peppers had painted on the floor. This permitted the automobiles to have an attractive appearance. Each team member was clean, shiny, "Gassed up and ready to roll," was one of Redd Peppers most often used replies to Mr. Uppity.

Redd was at his desk nestled in a corner of the cavernous room deeply engrossed in a catalog of auto accessories. When he heard Golly Gee coming across the concrete floor, with her hard heels clacking a unique rhythm and her starched uniform swishing to the beat of her walk, he looked up with that big, white toothy grin of his that was always gleaming. His eyes clear, and alert. They blinked from recognition of Golly and flashed an innocent sky blue. His cheeks had a Scottish rosy glow both summer and winter. They sometimes looked chapped but only signaled a healthy blood supply. A type of unceasing boyish blush. All of this was topped off by a grand growth of classic red hair with a mind of its own. His hair stood up in places and slept in places.

He stood with a greeting as Golly reached the desk area. "Golly, it is so nice to see you this morning. A very busy one I am sure."

His shoulders seemed too large for his jacket as he reached out his big, paw for a handshake. His Scottish cheeks blushed a deeper hue. She returned the compliment and a glow of her own.

Redd offered Golly the padded, straight back chair that she had used many times before. Settling in, she pulled the chair immeasurably closer and began the conversation by saying, "I feel that the days ahead will be full and very complicated."

She elaborated about the Smidgen's early morning flight.

"Some guests are coming this day about the sale of Rustic Realm. Our little Smidgens are on a flight to see what they could see in the lawn and wood area. We hope they come back safe and with some good report."

She also gave Redd the mood and ambience of the Mansion in general. "The general mood in the Mansion is still somber. A feeling of hopelessness has evolved about the Uppitys. The sale of the mansion would seem to signify the end of hoping for the return of little Jump."

They quickly and professionally spoke with each other at length about the day's activities and other relevant events. Keep me informed of any changes in the actions of the pending buyers. We need to keep on top of this whole sale thing. Not only for our jobs but also for the possible finding of Jump. I have to prepare for a luncheon and Bakka is making the menu with care and skill, but with a certain amount of sadness. When all was said and done the two parted. Good friends at all times.

Golly returned to the house to again take up the managing of the cleaning project and to see to other household duties. Cleaning floors and walls were the easy parts. Taking down beds and mattresses and airing them outside was one of the hard parts. The drapes and curtains would get cleaned and dusting was never ending.

Redd began to get the big 1975 Cadillac ready. His task was to fetch Mr. Uppity and the realtor, a Mr. Snooty, for the house. He was to bring them and possibly a buyer for the property back to view the estate.

Golly, Bakka and Redd went about their duties with dread about the future of Rustic Realm. The sale of their home would mean many changes.

Bakka was cooking up a storm to furnish the luncheon guests with the best she had to offer. Redd was giving the car one last shine and window cleaning. Even so, the two Smidgens were still on their minds.

Redd jumped into the big Caddy and pushed the button to open the garage door in front of the car. As the door slowly opened, with only a faint hum, Redd started the fine automobile and slowly moved out onto the drive and then down the lane to the road.

Chapter

FIVE

The trusty machine purred with a steady advance upon the road that headed to the city. Redd went to the factory's offices where Mr. Uppity had his headquarters, and parked around in back after informing the gatekeeper of his arrival.

Redd was notified via the car phone that Mr. Uppity was ready and Redd was to come to the front entrance. "I am ready to be picked up Redd. Please come around to the front so I can exit."

Redd eased the big Caddy along the executive building and around and up to the granite steps that decorated the front portals of Mr. Uppity's office building. It was an imposing building with much glass and decorative shutters on the windows. The exterior was brick and stone that gave the whole appearance of wealth and stability.

In a few minutes, Mr. Empire Uppity came out through the big glass front door that had been opened for him by one of his many loyal employees and headed for the car. Upon sighting him, Redd was out of the cooled car and at attention to open the car door for his employer.

Mr. Uppity was a tall man with a mass of salt and pepper gray hair as his crown. The years before Jump came up missing had been good to him and it still showed. Empire was still a handsome man. With skin still tight and few wrinkles about his face, he could be taken for a man ten years his junior. He was thin and had no paunch. His forehead intelligent but creased with worry. His shoulders bent forward a little, expressing the weighty burdens of his sorrow and of his leadership responsibilities. His eyebrows were bushy and protected what had once been deep blue- eyes now a kind of watery blue. Each eye had an old set of crow's feet on the side to remind him of happier, smiley days gone by. His nose was aristocratic. His mouth was thin and these days unsmiling most of the time. Nevertheless, he is a good man.

He climbed into the backseat with a sigh, closed the door, and gave the orders on how and where to pick up Mrs. Uppity.

Redd knew every corner and bump and how to get through the lights by timing them in advance. Redd was famous for his gentle, smooth, big city, auto ride. Just as Redd pulled up to, the large, gray stone building that housed Mrs. Mater Uppity's charity Mission of Mercy. A charity that ministered to young people that needed help in schooling. Books, school supplies and even teachers were supplied by her charity. Most of those were in countries of the third world. Mr. Uppity informed Redd to be prepared to pick up three more passengers later after picking up Mrs. Uppity.

A movement at one of the gray curtains from one of the gray windows of the charity's building signaled that there was life inside. The building was unimposing and gave no indication of the good work that went on inside. A few moments later, Mrs. Uppity appeared at the front door and glided down the steps and into the car. Mrs. Mater Uppity was a regal lady of attractive bearing. Small and frail by modern standards. Short, gray hair with a face that was still lovely. Intelligent forehead and dancing eyes and she still had her girlish figure. It was still a pleasure to look at her. A few quiet tender greetings and then words of information. "Redd, we want you to go downtown to the Snooty real estate offices. You should know were it is." Redd replied in the affirmative.

Redd could see in the rearview mirror that thin and frail face of the car's newest occupant. She was the daughter of farm parents and knew hard work and disappointment. She was petite by today's standards, looking frail, but could work and fight big for her family by any standard.

Today she looked washed out. Her narrow shoulders hunched forward with her hands fidgeting on her lap, smoothing out unseen wrinkles on her dress. Her head hung down ever so slightly in a poise of humility and exhaustion. She wore a broad-rimmed hat that almost covered her premature, gray hair. She could still smile, but it was only forced on and appeared wearisome.

During her earlier years, she tried to have a child of

her own; Mater was the picture of wholeness and health. Even when the doctors began to abandon hope for her chances, her eyes would still sparkle at any talk about children and her smile appeared to be impossible to erase. The loss of Jump was a tragedy too heavy to keep hidden only in her heart. Jump was the child she always wanted. He is a boy with a great depth of need as well as being able to bestow love and affection. Jump came from a family wiped out by a terrible auto accident. No relatives came forward to offer to raise the lad. When he was put up for adoption, Mater heard of his plight and came to his rescue by adoption. It was to help him and to fulfill her desire for a family.

Redd effortlessly guided the big car into the parking lot of the Snooty Real Estate offices. Mr. Uppity got out hesitantly and went into the office. After a short time, he emerged with one Mr. Snooty and two prospective buyers for Rustic Realm. Redd was already out of the car and had both doors opened for the arriving occupants. Down came the two buyers into the car, causing Mrs. Uppity to sit on the edge of back seat. Mr. Snooty would sit on a jump seat that folded down and faced the back. Mr. Uppity would ride up front with Redd. This was a rare seating arrangement for an unusual day. Mr. and Mrs. Pinching were the epitome of courtesy and grace as they eked out pleasantries to one and all. Mrs. Penelope Pinching was thin and boney to the point of making crackling noises as she moved about. Her hawk-like face was pinched and milky white. Mr. Flinch Pinching was tall and gangly. His suit looked to be several sizes too large for his angular body "Its so nice to see you

Mrs. Uppity. I am sure the weather has been good at the mansion as it has been here in the city."

Mater Uppity gave a nod and a "yes" as her answer.

Mr. Pinching bent forwards and directed his remark to Empire Uppity, "how's business, Mr. Uppity?"

Empire with a strained smile answered,"OK"

Mr. Snooty wanted to talk on the way back to the mansion and talk he did. His was non-stop nervous chatter. His hands and body moving in a flailing motion like swimming things in the water. "It is such a nice day to be out in the country, don't you think? This parcel of land and the mansion will make a nice place to entertain as well as being secluded." No nosy neighbors or traffic to mar ones quiet time. Just look at the sky out here. The trees keep the air fresh is what my daddy always said. Mr. Pinching, just imagine you with a few horses out here in the country. Mrs. Pinching, you will be the envy of all your friends at the mansion to give parties and such." On and on Mr. Snooty extolled the virtues of this property. Most of the rambling seemed to Redd to be for the ears of Mr. Uppity to make the sale more plausible.

CHAPTER
SIX

edd Peppers pulled off the main road onto the property and was told to go slow by Mr. Snooty as the salivating realtor began to point out all the features of Rustic Realm to the hungry, apparent eager buyers.

Mr. Snooty previously had researched the property, and had on several occasions made trips up and around the driveway without prior consent. Only telling the Uppitys after Redd Peppers recognized him on one occasion. Evidently, he had taken many notes. Eventually he talked the Uppitys into selling, thereby leaving their sad memories behind. He craftily presented all of the pleasant possibilities of selling the Mansion and lands.

"You can both leave all this sadness behind if you sell and move. Now, without a young one on the property all of the amenities would go the waste. You would be happier in another climate or neighborhood. So many memories can cause one to be burdened beyond one's ability. Now is a good time to sell because the market is quite active. You will probably make a nice profit as well." Only smoke and mirrors were missing.

His face was long and lean. His black hair was slicked down, almost touching his beady eyes. His aquiline nose and sharp chin, rose and fell like a pair of scissors as he rambled on, with pseudo authority. He had a glib tongue, and oily movements, like an eel going down a wet riverbank.Mr.Snooty was stressful to look at thought, Mrs. Uppity.

Slowly up the drive the big Caddy moved as each bush and flower were pointed out with a long bony finger. Mr. Snooty took a deep breath as he turned to the mansion and began to point to the height and breadth of the mansion itself. He was still chattering away as Redd pulled up to the front door of the mansion and allowing all of the little party to disembark.

"Isn't it beautiful and charming? The plantings are superb as well as the lawns. Just look at the expanse. One can visualize all kinds of games and entertainment on theses grounds."

Mr. Snooty oozed out of the vehicle last and exclaimed with his out-stretched boney limbs, "Isn't this magnificent?"

Redd was told by Mr. Uppity to return to the garage and wait for instructions to return to the city in an hour or so. He would contact Redd by the house phone. Redd gave a nod and a "Yes sir" as he noticed how sad and small Mrs. Uppity seemed as she almost stumbled into the house.

Redd returned to the garage were he would clean the car inside and out and check it over stem to stern. Cleaning the interior as well as the car's shiny exterior was Redd's duty and joy.

Just as he started into the garage, he again noticed Peyton coming from the grape arbor and wondered what he was doing there. Peyton was heading for the kitchen. He was walking slowly, without any vim or vigor. "Tired, old cat looks like he might be getting up in years," Redd muttered as he turned back to his own affairs.

Bakka called Redd on the intercom line and was told that she had made a pleasant little tea lunch for the party of five but had enough to share with him. She would be glad to bring it down to him after serving the guests and before their return to the city. Redd was glad and answered, "thanks, I am certainly hungry after my trip into town."

Redd hoped Snooty was not very good at his job. It also seemed to Red that the sell was overdone by Snooty. More gab than was needed, as the Pinchings seemed to be sold already.

CHAPTER
SEVEN

Bakka Beans always enjoyed the company of Golly Gee, but most of the time the two ladies were so busy that it was difficult to be very sociable with long conversations. Therefore, it was that morning of the big meeting with Mr. Snooty and a couple that wants to buy the property that Golly came through Bakka's kitchen.

"Got to run Bakka. I have still a lot of things to do this day as I know you have too."

Bakka knew this was a true statement, knowing all of the culinary requirements she also needed to accomplish.

Lunch would be light but tasty. It would be in two parts. Fruit and Vegetables with dip followed by chicken croquettes. All of the extra help hired to clean the house, plus some of the staff, would break at noon as custom dictated. Most of the extra help came out from town once each year. Three ladies and two men made all the difference in the world to get the big job done. Bakka was told to expect six people for a little afternoon lunch later, the Uppitys, and three persons involved in the sale of real estate.

The cleaning of the house was practically finished by then and the extra help would go to their homes, leaving the regular staff and Golly and Bakka.

Bakka worked out all of the details and the menu the day before with Mater, to be certain everything was perfect.

Bakka sang or talked to herself as she whirled around the kitchen, opening drawers, wielding many utensils, and in a hundred motions, preparing good things with the flair on a concert pianist. Bakka was a happy person with black hair and twinkling eyes full of mirth and compassion. Slightly rotund and short of stature she was not someone you would miss in a crowded room, because of her magnetic personality. Once in a while she passed by a small mirror hung over her little desk and peeked at herself to be sure she looked as good as she cooked.

The special lunch this afternoon was especially for the prospective buyers and Mr. Snooty. Snooty was here once before and liked bland and tasteless things, Bakka thought. Custards, creams, cheese spread, and pureed meats with lots of catsup on white bread with the crust cut off were more to his liking. She planned to have iced tea and lemonade. Whole-wheat crackers and vegetables with dip were the order of the day. In addition, some of those little sandwiches with meat and pimento cheese would round out her menu. Maybe, she could put in a smidgen of Texas hot sauce to tweak the taste buds of Mr. Snooty.

She always kept the crusts to make sandwiches for the Smidgens; they loved the crusts, especially the Bright Ones. She had convinced them that the crusts kept their hair shiny, lively, and curly. Just what her mother had told her years before. Early this morning, Bakka prepared the lunches for Fidget and Fussy and used the bread crusts to make an adequate number of mini, mouth watering, and finger licking treats. Roast beef was the favorite of the Bright Ones.

Bakka put in some sweet pickle slices; celery sticks with peanut butter, and grapes to top off a fine spring lunch for the Smidgens while on their flight. She reminded herself when she reached into a drawer for some flatware, the first time she saw the Smidgens. There, behind the drawer rested some of the micro knives, forks, and spoons that she kept washed and ready when some special meals she served up to the eager and usually hungry Smidgens.

The first time she saw the small utensils, earlier, she excitedly asked Golly to whom they belonged. "What is the tiny flatware used for, she asked."

"You will not believe what I have seen in our mansion," replied Golly.

'Well, tell me any way because I will believe you."

"There is a small group of little people that have taken up residence in the mansion's upper floors. I caught one last winter when the temperature went down to 20 below. An old one, named Graybub, who was the leader, told me of their plight and I agreed to shepherd them indoors for as long as needed."

Bakka had a hard time believing it then. Later Bakka

sought some solitude upstairs in the solarium. While Bakka sat there quietly considering the events and joys of her life, she noticed out of the corner of her eye some movement. Slowly turning her head, not to disturb the moment she was startled to see something few people had ever seen.

A sleek mouse was scampering in and around the plants on the shelves. To make this sight even more unbelievably was the addition of a tiny personage riding on its back as though it was a horse. This was the first time Bakka had seen a Smidgen, but it was not to be her last.

Bakka with her mouth agape and her hands clutching her heart couldn't speak for both joy and surprise. She had heard about Little People when she was younger and had hoped they existed. This then, was her joy in this sighting.

To find them in the in the mansion, riding mice was her surprise.

When she finally composed herself, she tried to follow them but to no avail. No mice, no Smidgen in sight. As she ran to find Golly, she reminded herself that the sight of the romping mice didn't cause her any fright or fear. Only surprise. Maybe it was because she was in a contemplative frame of mind. When she found Golly, she had a hundred questions that eventually were all answered.

Guess what I just saw?

Golly looked at her friend and answered, "well, tell me before you burst."

"I just saw some of the little people you had described to me earlier. What a surprise and joy.

"Did you see them in the solarium?"

"Yes. And they were riding some mice as though they were ponies."

"Well, you have seen your first Smidgens but I assure you not the last."

Now Bakka could join Redd and Golly to enjoy, care, and protect these lovable little, folks.

Bakka breezed through the regular lunch and now she began setting up for the afternoon tea. She looked out the window and saw the sun in a position to suggest that the party of five would soon be on the scene. Cocking her ear to one side, she was able to determine that a big car was coming up the driveway and soon several car doors slammed shut to confirm the arrival of the troupe.

It was just a few minutes later that Redd called on the house phone to confirm his arrival and to request some food be brought down to the garage for him, if feasible.

Bakka hung up the phone and sat down to examine her list to be sure all of her duties had been performed. She waited to be called by the Uppitys to serve her tea.

She could hear them walking through the house and opening and closing doors. Mr. Snooty occasionally emitted a forced laugh but no other voice was heard in the serious business of merchandising ones house and home. The Uppitys had given the staff the impression that they were very hesitant about the whole affair.

Eventually, a call came and Mrs. Mater Uppity informed Bakka to serve. Bakka came right away and pushed open the French doors that led to the patio and with a whirl and a smile, brought out the tea fixings on an ornate tray to the center of the patio table. There were soft sounds of admiration and appreciation at the elegant presentation of this afternoon repast by the beaming Bakka Beans.

"Ah," and "yum," were mouthed with genuine appreciation.

A few words of thanks and some of inquiry were exchanged by the ladies as Bakka busied herself in the pouring of the liquids into fine goblets, and arranging the napkins and other flurries of activity she always did at eating time. Bakka went to the serving cart and rearranged lemon wedges and other dainties in a stalling maneuver. Her ears being cocked to catch any news or other tidbits that would be of interest to Golly or the staff. After hearing, nothing interesting she excused herself for other chores but assured Mater she would be available if needed.

When returning to the kitchen, she took with her some surplus sugar cubes and lemons. She really had her hands full as she opened the French door and entered the large family room that was darkened by shades and drapes.

Her shoe found the edge of a throw rug in this subdued light. Almost in slow motion she reached out to catch the arm of a large chair to break her fall only to see the lemons and sugar cubes go in all different directions. Her fall ended abruptly but with out any trauma. Bakka was embarrassed and quickly looked about, ready to see whether anyone had witnessed her little accident. She was pleased no telling eye had seen her.

She slowly regained her composure and on hands and knees began looking for her spilled items. Slowly one by one she retrieved the little treasures, and they were now placed more prudently in her giant apron pockets.

After a while, all except one of the lemons had been found and tucked safely away. As she diligently sought that one last lemon, she carefully worked towards the partially opened French Doors only to hear the complicated conversation of the three men on the patio.

Bakka cautiously began to arise from her position on her knees to determine what was being said as well as done. Her knees cracked but not enough for an alarm to the group of five.

Mr. Snooty had spread a map on the table. Snooty, Mr. Uppity and Mr. Pinching put some of their lunch on the serving cart. The three men hovered over the old engineers map and were discussing some very interesting things.

"Just look how much land is included in the property?"

"Several hundred acres. I've not seen this particular map," commented Mr. Uppity as he ran his finger over the faded lines.

Mr. Pinching was making sounds of contentment as he moved back a ways and related his approval, "It is just what we want for our very own estate."

Bakka was in a quandary about eavesdropping and being so very secretive. In any other situation she thought, she should just walk away and retrieve her lemon at some other opportune time. There were friends involved in such a complicated manner in these doings, she thought that listening in would benefit more than hurt. Redd Peppers, Golly Gee, Mr. Brown, and all of the Smidgens all could benefit by knowing what is going on. If this property was sold each and everyone mentioned would be impacted by a loss of employment or a safe haven to have as a home.

As the three men scrutinized the map carefully, Mr. Uppity asked Mr. Snooty "What does this penciled in square mean? It is in the corner of our property that is in the deep woods. I thought we owned that far into the woods," asked Mr. Uppity with authority

Mr. Snooty nervously cleared his throat and said," about ten years ago, before you bought Rustic Realm, I sold a little parcel of land apart of the original large estate with the permission of the former owner. I had completely forgotten about it until I was reminded by this map," he continued in a highly strained voice.

"The former owner of Rustic Realm needed some cash in haste and didn't know they would be selling it to you in just a short time later. Therefore, when a couple from Strangeville wanted to buy that little piece of land way back in the deep woods the former owner said to me, "go ahead, sell it." Mr. Snooty rubbed his thin chin and continued. "It's coming back to me now." His eyes squinted as though in pain. "That land was situated on a weed infested fire road to get in and out. It was unfit for regular travel. It was also choked with trees and bushes. The Strangeville couple said it would be all right with them and so we settled on a price. They paid for it in cash and that was the last time I remember seeing them. It was said a little later by the realtor grapevine that a small house was built on the land. With no news or reports in recent years, I had completely forgotten about the whole transaction, when we sold the estate to you," Mr. Snooty continued, "It had not yet been put on this map by the county engineer. I thought I had told you something about a little parcel being sold-off way back in the deep woods."

Mr. Uppity thought it could have slipped his mind too.

Mr. and Mrs. Pinching had remained very quiet during this discourse but felt it was time to interject some timely comments.

Casually discounting the plot of ground in the deep woods, they hoped to change the subject. Mr. Pinching commented, "I don't need that little piece of ground, and it makes no difference to us that it was sold off years ago".

Mr. Pinching was now standing as he spoke and wanted his wife to chime in her affirmation. She nodded her approval with a big toothy grin and went back to her lemonade, complementing the sourness of the drink. "This is certainly is a fine lemonade, made from real lemons, no doubt."

Mr. and Mrs. Pinching indicated that they liked the property and wanted to buy it immediately for their own home. "We like all of the things about Rustic Realm and wish to buy it just as soon as it was convenient to both Mr. and Mrs. Uppity." "The price seems about right," Added Mr. Pinching said under his breath, but loud enough for Empire to hear.

Bakka could see that the intensity of the moment had faded and that she should get back to the kitchen where she really belonged. Bakka looked down at the door opening and saw the missing lemon. While still standing inside the family room unseen by the tea party, she proceeded to retrieve the yellow fruit. She knelt down and slowly reached out through the door crack and to the edge of the patio, to retrieve the lonely lemon.

Just as she grasped the yellow citrus orb, she looked up to find that Mater Uppity's eyes met hers. Mater looked surprised, yet faintly smiled with understanding and imperceptibly nodded in recognition.

Peyton had quietly entered the patio and caused Mater to look down from her table setting. Mater quickly turned her stoic face, and eyes back to the little group.

As Bakka drew in her hand with the captured lemon through the small opening at the French doors so did a black blur of fur. That bit of movement caused Bakka to be discovered by Mater but not betrayed. That cat seemed to cause more trouble than he was worth. Bakka returned to the kitchen with everything, including her dignity.

Bakka now back in her own kitchen where she had to share it with that black cat who was busy eating out of his bowl the delightful food set out earlier for him. While washing her hands, she thought of the cat and his place here in Rustic Realm. Her conclusion, Peyton was certainly a pain.

Bakka quickly but with careful motions assembled another tray filled with good things for her fellow staff member, Redd, loved BLTs and salads with croutons. She hurried with the tray to the garage. She met Redd who was coming to see what was the delay. "I can only stay a minute and must get back to the kitchen," she said as she handed over the tray and food. "If you see Golly Gee, tell her that when I can get the time I'll share with both of you what I have learned," she said as she turned about in a rush to return to the house.

Redd scratched his red hair and took the tray laden with tasty food the garage and his desk where he ate hungrily.

The call came to bring the Caddy around to the front because the guests were planning to leave. In only fifteen minutes, Redd was gently moving down the driveway to the big city with three very excited and talkative dealmakers. Mr. Snooty reached forward to close the glass partition in the limo, separating Redd from his passengers.

Redd was alone with his thoughts as he drove and no new news to give his friends. Since Jump had been missing Redd knew that his employment was in jeopardy because of the Uppitys desire to live some place else. A place where a chauffeur would not be needed. He would be separated from his fellow employees as well as all of the Smidgens. He was especially concerned about the Smidgens and their future in this entire annoying scenario.

CHAPTER
EIGHT

When Fidget tried unsuccessfully to call out in a whisper for one or more of the mice that might be in the vicinity, he decided to try to whistle in the special way he had learned from the elders. Touching his front teeth with two fingers at the gum line and gently pushing in with his curled tongue, he blew hard. This produced a high-pitched note, unheard by human ears and would permeate the area and mobilize mice towards the whistler.

The whistle indicated that one or two of the Smidgens would like a ride. Fussy was right at his shoulder warning him to be careful because of Peyton might be on the prowl. Eventually, two of their mice friends, Nibbles and Twitch were in the room, cautiously looking about for the source of the special whistle sent out to alert them of a Smidgen in need.

The mice spied their two little friends on the top of the glider. Then the mice scurried up the cloth side and on to the cushions to accommodate the whistler and his companion.

In a moment, the reunion was complete, and the Bright Ones had saddled the mice and put all their gear on the backs of the two little helpers, freeing the two moths to do whatever giant moths do.

Fidget was out front again and giving orders to Fussy to wait in the room until he signaled that all was clear. Holding tight the reins, he urged his little rodent, Twitch, to begin the sortie to the back of the house where the other Smidgens would be. Out of the Solarium and into the hallway Twitch moved cautiously. His little paws holding onto to the hallway rug, he made the advance in small jerky motions.

Fidget would give the all clear to the waiting Fussy when the way was safe. At that moment, he saw out of the corner of his eye what he thought was a little white flag waving. In a flash, the white flag exposed itself as a coiled black body of destruction coming straight at the twosome. The silent furry form was high in the air proceeding with teeth bared, and claws extended. It was Peyton in all of his menacing terror.

Fidget was no stranger to danger and knew the moves that were taught by the Elders, to avoid the Peyton threat.

Pulling the reins sharply to the right, he piloted the mouse to the wall. They both hit the wall with a faint thud and nearly tumbled over. He saw stars suddenly appear to be present everywhere, with dizzy rotating ceilings in need of correction. Fidget shook his head to bring back the scene before him to properly deal with the snarling peril.

Fidget felt like an egg in front of a steamroller. In the very same second, that this was happening the cat was sailing through the air with fangs and eyes set on a two-course meal before him. In mid air he began to squirm and jerk to reset his sights for his targets new position for the two travelers had moved slightly. Then Peyton's' eyes grew to twice their regular size when he realized this correction would put him at odds with the wall before him.

The fraction of a second before contact, the flying feline's nervous system seemed to explode into disorientation. He hit the wall head first with a painful thud. The entire jumbled mass of fur fell to the floor in a disorganized heap. The little-dazed duo, Fidget and Twitch, that had been at the walls edge waiting for the cat to hit the wall, found themselves surrounded by an enemy's gasp of catnip breath and four immobilized legs.

Both mouse and Smidgen now fully recovered from the head bumps to the cats frightening presence. Taking a deep breath they kept perfectly still while Fidget formulated a plan of action. Fidget saw that the big menace was out like a decked prizefighter.

He immediately called to Fussy to hurry on while the big cat was being counted out, to at least a ten count. Mouse Twitch jumped over the sprawled out legs of Peyton and delayed for a second while Nibbles, Fussy's mouse, and Fussy caught up to them. The foursome moved very quickly down the hall and into one of the back bedrooms used for storage. The room had been appointed their meeting place when they returned.

"We will meet in the storage room after our flight to reveal what we had observed", still rang in the ears of the two bright Ones when they said it earlier.

In just a few moments, all of the Smidgens were reunited with the Bright Ones, and hugs and smiles were everywhere. Fidget could tell they had interrupted a very serious meeting of the elders and others that wanted to air their concerns about leaving the mansion. No one would continue until the travelers had told them of their adventure.

"We flew high in the morning air to view all of the beautiful grounds and landscape of Rustic Realm. We had a nice picnic on the grape arbor and watched Peyton do his thing from our safe perch. We returned just now and had a close call with the cat in the hallway but as you can see we escaped unscathed," said Fidget

Fussy added, "we flew as high as the moths could go and saw deep in the woods and," she stopped not wanting to reveal any details about the smoke from the chimney from the little blue-green house. She continued, "and other beauties in the stream and freshly tilled fields".

After telling most of the traveling details, as well as their recent encounter with Peyton, Fidget and Fussy turned the meeting back to the elders (Graybub and Oldene) and the matter under discussion. Fidget and Fussy thought that the detail about the little blue-green house in the deep woods would wait until after they told Golly Gee, privately.

The Elders had agreed that they had fulfilled their commitment to Golly Gee of living just in the house in the winter. Graybub expounded, "The dangers of the outside were no greater than those of the mansion. In addition, the encounter with Peyton, which Fidget and Fussy just, had proved their point. A few years ago when Peyton came on the scene, Golly Gee had insisted that we come in from the yard and garden area. She added that the severe winters and chemical pollutants as well as diminishing acceptable habitat was good enough reason to spend the winter in-doors. In the house, she helped us avoid the fatal feline's frolicking in the yard. The cat appears playful sometimes, but when no one is looking the natural kitty has deadly tendencies. Only when Jump came to live at the mansion has Peyton's activities mellowed into a moderate quality. The cat mellowed to Jump in a big way. Peyton was always near Jump and purring like a motorboat. At night, the big cat found himself at the foot of Jump's little bed keeping the boy's feet warm."

It was noted that Golly Gee was good to her promise of help and protection all this time, and no accident had befallen the Smidgens. In the old days, the Smidgens lived mostly outdoors under old trees, leaves, bushes, logs, stumps, and the like, even living under giant toadstools. Inside they have enjoyed high places in clothing, closets and coo coo clocks, behind pictures and even in the walls with the mice. These clever places of convenience made their detection and purging very difficult. Now, after a hard winter, the yearning to return to the great outdoors was too strong to discount. They all wanted to take a vote this spring, before bringing it up to Golly Gee, so that they would be more unified. They didn't want to take 'no' for an answer this time.

"No more living in that old Grandfather clock all winter and listening to it strike every hour and quarter hour until your head rings," old Crinkle said.

"I never did get used to that scratchy wool fabric," said another.

Graybub and Oldene, the two elders older than dirt but still the head of the clan, also added some negative comments for good measure. These two as husband and wife spoke in unison. "The confine of a house causes one to feel cramped and breathless sometimes."

"Lets take a vote," proposed old Crinkle. Therefore, they did.

The vote to return to the great outdoors won handily, twenty to sixteen. It was decided to tell Golly Gee just as soon as possible. Most of the older Smidgens wanted to return outdoors. Fidget and Fussy where disappointed with the turn of events hoping for a more unanimous consensus but knew that they needed help from Golly to plan and execute their pending flight over the blue-green house in the deep woods as soon as possible. There was something about the house that called to mind the kidnapping of Jump. A little house in the deep woods. No one knew it existed. A place not searched by the authorities gave way to suspicions especially by the Bright Ones. They would talk to Golly shortly, before too much changed with a sale of the property.

After the meeting broke up, it was time for the two Bright Ones to unpack their gear and settle in with their friends and relatives. Fidget and Fussy, unpacking their little back packs, were enjoying being the center of attention at the end of the day. They were so excited, that all their friends knew that the trip of the high flight was special. It was difficult not to talk about the blue-green house, but it was known that false hopes were not to be encouraged at this time. Some of their friends were now lacking earlier timidly and voiced a desire to fly high also.

Ever since the meeting this afternoon, all the Smidgens seemed to be more courageous than ever before. Fidget and Fussy explained that the trip was so exhausting that most of the regular moths would not be able to take that strenuous flight."

"Our two trained moths made the trip without exhaustion because of our training, grooming, and feeding our mounts. You would find it unrewarding using the smaller and less experienced moths."

That didn't seem to matter very much to the other young Smidgens gathered around the Bright Ones, because soon all of them would be free to go outdoors and travel as they pleased as it had been in earlier days, they thought. As the night unraveled, the Smidgens left one by one and went their own way to retire. Sleep began to grow heavy on Fidget and Fussy also, so it was that each went to the new places of their family residences, to rest and refresh themselves for the days ahead. They went to the attic space bedrooms that were now full of clothes not needed by the Uppitys this summer as it gave the Clan new places to reside. A few days slipped by with nothing unusual to deal with.

This morning came sunny and hopeful. Mr. sun peeked over the rolling hills with his orange-red fire penetrating the clear country air. A new day waited with its excitement and drama ready to unfold as the players began one by one to awake to the sights and sounds of the brilliant spring morning.

The Smidgens started to gather from their unique places of repose, to the Solarium on the third floor. Some came from behind pictures, closet shelves, grandfather clocks, tissue boxes, clothing, and many other secretive locations.

The room was all a-buzz with the news of the past several days. Eventually the council members started to bring the gathering to order with "hush and quiet."

Old Graybub commenced to speak to the attended company, because he was the eldest of the elders. "It's time to return to the great out doors that our forefathers knew and loved. The severity of the weather has moderated, and spraying for bugs has dwindled to insignificant levels. These and other dangers have diminished to acceptable levels. All of us have become accustomed to the perils of the big cat both indoors and out," he said authoritatively. "Even with the Peyton's advancing years we all must remain diligent and careful inside and out. Our tactics to avoid and outwit the furry beast have prevailed but its time we took back our beloved trees and stumps, bushes and mushrooms. We all love Golly Gee and her friends, the cook and chauffeur. Her infinite care and love have been most appreciated. She has, without reservation, taught us more about the BIG world than any of us ever hoped to know. Redd Peppers has been like a Father to many of us with his wisdom and can never be replaced." Clearing his throat and stroking his white beard for effect, he went on.

"Let us choose a committee to approach Golly Gee and tell her of these intentions and ask for her blessings. It is imperative that we agree, and harmony of relationships are maintained."

Graybub finished his speech with one final tug of his beard. Some of the more conservative and sedate Smidgens pushed for caution and slow, deliberate action, such as Flippant. Flippant, a young adult with negative views on most things is always complaining. He said, "I don't like changes and the outdoors is full of unknowns. My hope is we stay right here."

Ultimately, a committee was elected and given the task to contact Golly Gee and acquaint her with the feelings of the group. Fussy was one of those selected to represent the young ones and their views. Graybub's wife, Oldene, was chosen to present a mature and moderate viewpoint. Flippant was chosen for his negative side of the change. "I don't think we should change our living quarters to the outside because it is too dangerous and cold in the winter. Dogs and cats as well as birds of prey on the branches of trees is not my idea of a safe and cozy place to live," proclaimed Flippant pompously.

This meeting eventually disbanded, and the Committee of three stayed to finalize a time and place to have their meeting. Opinions agreed that it should be convened immediately. Oldene assumed the position of chairperson and proposed that they try to find Golly as soon as possible and not delay any longer in this discussion.

Today, at this hour, Golly would be in the kitchen having a cup of coffee with Bakka Beans. The event of spring house cleaning earlier would be the topic of discussion. It would be a quiet time because the Uppitys had gone to town earlier with Redd Peppers. Three mice were called and came scurrying from their secret hiding places to carry the committee.

The Committee silently rode off down the hall passageway, hugging close to the baseboard. It was a fluid and uneventful trip as it had been reported that Peyton was seen going outside and slinking towards the Grape Arbor.

When they neared the kitchen, the voices of the two ladies could be discerned. The Committee dismounted the mice and dismissed the little gray creatures to return to their regular activities of looking for food and finding places of concealment in the walls.

Oldene tiptoed into the room and made sure of its availability by slowly looking in all directions before attempting to walk into the room unannounced. The only two persons in the room were Golly Gee and Bakka Beans talking quietly about the flight of the two bright ones. Oldene prepared to be recognized by staying close to the wall, in case the giant participants would inadvertently step on them.

Oldene chose to take her cane and tap it to be signal. And TAP she did. The end of her old crooked cane struck one the lower cabinet doors, and it sounded like the drums of deepest Africa. The two ladies in conversation immediately stopped in mid sentence. They were more startled than frightened.

This sound had happened many times before and both ladies knew instinctively that Oldene was on the scene "Well look who is here. You three are welcome to come up on the table if you accept my hand," said Golly with sincerity and warm hospitality in her voice.

Some spoons were turned over to make seats for them

to sit upon. A few pots were always placed strategically around the table for a barrier and protection from any prying eyes. The three Smidgens all were greeted and jumped upon the overturned spoons. Each one was bursting with information, and it took Oldene to bring the meeting to order with her strong, raspy voice.

Oldene was younger than she appeared. The years had been hard on her. She had spent many years on the outside and had skin that accommodated that type of existence. Her skin was bronzed and wrinkled from cold blowing wind. Her forehead was intelligently high and her chin narrow. Her eyes were small but clear and betrayed her, occasionally, by displaying humor and empathy. It was thought her old grouchy ways were just a put on, a mask to appease Graybub.

Golly, out of respect, let Oldene have her way even though she was desirous to know more about Fussy's trip in the high atmosphere the day before. Fussy knew that, winked at Golly, and whispered, "later".

Oldene jumped up off of her spoon, stood at center stage, and began speak in a high pitched excited voice. Getting right to the point she began, "We had a meeting earlier where the subject of returning to the outdoors came up. The group seemed to be in favor of returning to the outdoor life we where accustomed to. We wanted to include you and Bakka in the decision process so that no hard feelings belong to anyone."

She continued by walking up and down the table, pounding her cane down, and throwing up her diminutive hands from time to time in a special fashion she was noted for. "We think it is time to once again enjoy the woods and stumps and trees like our forefathers before us enjoyed Some of us, I fear have become complacent and lazy enjoying your hospitality and indoor living.

After each conclusion, she would bend over slightly with her fists placed on her hips and look into the ladies eyes until she was sure the information was received.

Flippant sat on his spoon and sputtered with words to counter what Oldene had said but to no avail.

"We all want to return to the great outdoors." Oldene finally completed her dissertation and sat down with that satisfied look on her face that only comes from years of debating and winning. Her gray hair seemed whiter, and her wrinkles appeared deeper.

The two ladies asked, "How? Why? "When." Therefore, it continued t with Oldene giving a few short answers.

"We appreciate all you have done for us and would always remember the love and attention you both showered on us."

On the committee Flippant, a tightly wound fellow with apparent confidence issues, who was in disagreement. Flippant was a timid young man with safety and ease as high priorities in his life.

He began, "No change at this time, please. Not now." One by one, he took the older ones to task. "The older Smidgens just want to make the younger ones miserable with challenges and difficulties. The old days are gone, and a new day of ease is at hand, don't let us let it slip away. Not every Smidgeon wants to return to the outside."

Flippant stood erect in his cocky way and continued his dialogue while Bakka Beans eyes rolled back in her head and Golly kept wiping her brow. "Its just not right,

Its just not right. The older folks always want to make the younger ones miserable." When Flippant finally wound down and started to take a deep breath to continue, Golly interjected with a comment.

"And what does one of the Bright Ones say about all this moving?" Golly looked right past the red faced Flippant. Her adoring eyes drank in the intelligent and beautiful Fussy. What Golly Gee saw was an engaging and blossoming young lady who was the embodiment of all that was good with the Smidgens.

Fussy eyes immediately met those of Golly, and she took the initiative as an actress takes her cue. Jumping up with a 'Fussy Flip' of her hair and waving her arms, she began to speak like a machine gun.

"We want to return to our roots in the woods and garden outside. We would like some excitement in our lives while we are still young. The ease indoors verges on boring. Young people are meant to eventually try their wings at braving the struggles and overcoming the adversities of life."

Poor Flippant hadn't a chance. His deep breath went to waste. He sat down like a deflated balloon.

Fussy went on, "I remember when I was younger, the free movements in the great outdoors to explore and appreciate was exciting. I do thank Red and Bakka as well as Golly for all the things we have been taught while inside the mansion."

Fussy continued her dialogue with her arms oscillating and her smile flashing, complete with several more Fussy Flicks, "We need to return to our roots and experience the world as our forefathers did."

After all this talking it was decided that time was

needed to contemplate all of these suggestions. A review was to be made in a few days. It would be needed for clear heads to make a wise decision. Fussy was glad. Oldene was sad. Flippant was bad.

Oldene and Flippant said that they would return upstairs by calling for two of the mice and would await Golly's answer in a few days.

Fussy said she would like to stay and visit awhile and tell of her trip on the giant moth up in the higher layers of air. Bakka had to get up and begin food preparations. That left the two friends to talk and have their little meeting.

Fussy began by telling of all the exhilarating feelings and events that occurred while she and Fidget rode the big moths up and into the higher atmosphere. Golly Gee listened intently.

Fussy was excited. "What an adventure," said the young lady. To top it all off she eventually stopped to detail the few seconds that she experienced when the little blue-green house came into view. "The house was almost invisible in the forest canopy. It was shear luck we spotted it." She had asked a few discreet questions to some of the older Smidgens to see if any had seen a little house when outdoors wandering around. None of them remembered a little house in the deep woods when they all lived in the great outdoors, several years ago.

"Something inside me said that this blue-green house had something to do with the disappearance of Jump," Fussy said. "Someone was still there because I saw a tiny puff of smoke coming out of what looked like the chimney."

All of a sudden, the entire scene on the back patio

the day before all came flooding back to Golly as told to her by Bakka.

"The realtor had admitted that he forgot the sale of that piece of land ten years ago," Bakka had said. She told little Fussy all that had happened and what was said in that meeting on the back patio.

They began to put two and two together and came up with the theory that maybe Jump was taken to the house by some people who had lost their son. Besides, no one knew the little house in that deep place in the woods. Not even the planes flying overhead had spotted the unassuming, camouflaged dwelling.

"We have to go back and see for ourselves," said Fussy, her voice now quivering with excitement. Pacing on the tabletop she was holding her head high and chattering on about they wanted to fly again over the area. "How happy everyone would be again. Fidget and I want to fly over that house for a closer look to see if any evidence points to the likelihood of kidnappers or Jump's presence."

Finally, Golly Gee had to restrain her own optimism and coax Fussy back to the present realities. "Let's wait a few days before we do anything really radical or dangerous," Golly said. It was only then that they began to whisper, in anticipation of the secrecy needed.

We must not let the elders know we plan to fly again for they would be hesitant or unwilling to permit us to go," said Fussy.

I don't like to be misleading in our doings but you have a good point. I will make what arrangements that are necessary for you both to fly very soon. You both must be very careful. The flight seems to me to be dangerous for two young Smidgens. Preparations to go and return in one day must be observed to allay any questions about your whereabouts.

They discussed all the details of an adventure that would take Fussy and Fidget on a return flight to the deep woods and over the mysterious blue-green house. Each idea was thrashed about and looked at with a critical eye. Fussy wanted to extend the flight but Golly was against any extension of her abbreviated mission.

It was almost lunchtime when this meeting finally ended. Their feelings might be at a boil, but the plan was cool as a cucumber. Go, look, and return. That was the way, these two girls operated. They both thought, what a unique trip this would be to the blue-green house and its mystery.

Fidget waited with some impatience for the return of his companion. He had seen and spent some time with the two giant moths. Fidget brushed them and feed them as his duty dictated to keep the two moths in tiptop condition. They ended with just milling about on this lazy morning. Fidget left the moths to get an advantageous place to observe Fussy's return from downstairs. After a while, he saw two mice scurrying along the baseboard of the hallway with Oldene and Flippant mounted upon them. He stayed behind the clothes hamper in a closet, not wanting to reveal himself. He found it irksome to converse with Oldene and difficult to chat very long with Flippant. The mounted mice moved silently past Fidget's concealed observation post. They proceeded to one of the back rooms where many of the Smidgens liked to congregate on these warm spring days. Fidget kept his vigil knowing that only his friend, Fussy, would be able to fill him in fairly on all the details about the meeting.

After what seemed like an eternity, he noticed movement in the hallway and soon saw that it was Fussy, returning on foot to the Solarium where many of the Smidgens like to spend some of their spare time. Fidget gave out a whistle like a songbird and Fussy immediately stopped to see where the signal came from. Suddenly their eyes met and they both smiled.

With hand signals and head movements to indicate their next move, the two friends were soon reunited in the Solarium. Up in one of the large hanging planter pots, which was home to an air plant, the two settled down for a long talk. Fussy gave all the details of the meeting and what Golly Gee had said. She shared the plans of the house keeper and presented the time table that had been agreed upon. It wasn't long before both were unified with the plan and its details. "We are to fly the two moths in the daytime for a look-see over the blue-green house. We are to keep the particulars of the flight to ourselves. Golly indicated for us to fly, look, and return. We are to Locate the little blue-green house. Report on its surroundings. Then they must return. It was also imperative to procure supplies for one full day. We must do all of it without causing too much revelation to the clan concerning their dangerous plan.

The two embodied enough energy for a month of Sundays. They would wait at least a few days before trying to wing over the wooded lands to the mysterious blue-green house. This time would be used to prepare the Moths and to gather some of the supplies that would be needed on such a long flight. It was planned to start very early in the morning and return in the late afternoon.

They could accomplish all that was required in

daylight hours. They agreed to delay the adventure until Golly Gee determined a favorable weather report. She hoped all this would be affected before the real estate broker had any more interested buyers for the mansion. They felt that a big change in the whole situation here at Rustic Realm might influence the circumstances at the little blue-green House. That might upset any hope of discovering the hidden things. It was mutually agreed that secrecy would be in the best interest for the success of the trip.

CHAPTER
NINE

For a few days, the planned trip was built into reality little by little. The Moths were given extra rations of sugar water and flour. The two adventurers kept busy by adding small treasures to their back packs. Redd Peppers made little do-dads that could be used in emergencies. Miniature ropes and candles for light. Fidget was given a little shooter made out of rubber bands functioning much like a Scuba Diver's under water spear gun. Bakka Beans prepared little goodies that were dried and light. Little water bottles fashioned from an aluminum thimble.

Golly Gee made a map of the area based upon the one Bakka had seen on the patio. Finally all was accomplished and the day and hour were set by Golly according to the weather report. The night before the big flight, all of the interested and involved parties got together.

For perfection, a last big meeting was initiated. It was decided that the safest place to meet would be in the garage after most of the house had gone to bed. Golly, Redd, Bakka, Fidget and Fussy.

It was the habit of Mr. and Mrs. Uppity to retire early on Fridays to prepare for a big weekend in their life concerning the sale. This permitted the group to assemble in the garage at 10:00 Pm. They all gathered around Redd's big desk and began by friendly greetings, and then a spot of tea brought by Bakka. It was a pleasant balmy Spring evening, made so very exciting by the possibilities that tomorrow would bring.

Several high windows were open in the garage permitting the sounds of the evening to come in to mingle with the stimulating aura of the group. Somewhere a night bird sang to mate. Bats were on the wing to catch any insects that tried to offend the night atmosphere. The aroma of the hot beverage, mixed with the clean mechanic smells of the garage, only heightened the intrigue of this unlikely meeting.

Golly Gee was the logical spokesperson. "This is a very important flight because I have come to the conclusion that Jump may be kept prisoner in that blue-green house. Only a feeling really."

The meeting on the patio last week was reviewed in detail by Bakka and some conclusions given. Bakka and Redd would interject a comment or a viewpoint from time to time. Fussy and Fidget listened attentively and said very little. (Too excited?)

They agreed that early the next morning, Fidget and Fussy would saddle up Swoop and Glide. Moths would have their special goggles for daylight flight. Each

Smidgen would have their full day pack. They would fly down the back yard and over the small stream in the rear of the lawn area. The flight would continue to the right, following the stream into the woods and on to the glen area. Here, they would take a left turn over the plowed fields, parallel to a fence row that was next to the deep woods. Flying high so that the blue-green house could be seen, the Smidgens would turn left and begin the flight over the deep woods to the back side of the blue-green house.

They would make one pass over the house at the highest altitude possible for safety and then turn back to make a landing in the house's perimeter, at a place that seems most concealed. From that point they would ascertain who was inhabiting the house and what they were doing. A quick and cursory examination of the scene would be made to determine if Jump were there or had been in the vicinity. After accomplishing this extent of investigating it was impressed upon the scouts to return to home base to report their findings. No additional activity or intervention would be recommended at this time.

With each salient point that the big people made, the two little Smidgens nodded their heads in understanding and agreement. After all, once they were in flight they would be in control and command, captains of the atmosphere.

The time was fleeting by and it was noted that the two flyers would have to get up early. Therefore the meeting with all its plans and hopes was dissolved, and each one slowly dispersed, to return to their respective places of responsibilities. Each head was filled with the hope that the mission would be a revealing success.

All were convinced that the next day would help solve any unspoken problems that existed. Five hearts beat in such a way that surely they would touch many more, very soon. The plans had been made. The players were in place. The prayers had been said. Now sleep came hard. Ultimately, action would replace all the thinking and all the words of all the yesterdays.

Chapter

TEN

At first light, the Bright Ones had assembled in the solarium upstairs ready to go. A soft, gentle, upland breeze that refreshingly caressed the faces of two early risers came as an indication of favor. The two peered out the upstairs window and greeted the morning with confidence and determination. Darkness gave away very few secrets of the day to come. A few stars continued to wink, giving proof of the sky's existence.

Fidget and Fussy had been up before dawn, making preparations concerning all of the things needed for the flight. Saddlebags and light back packs filled to the brim with the minuscule necessities. Each had even packed some personal items. Flashlights, gum, trail mix, string, hankies, and small water bottles. The Bright Ones had envisioned the adventure much larger than others and more dangerous, there-by preparing for the flight very thoroughly and carefully. The two trusty moths had been feed and saddled without anyone suspecting exactly what the Bright Ones were going to do. It had been difficult not to tell any of their friends or kin about the dangerous flight. To do so would only cause more strife and dissension among the group. The fervor of each day's discussions was high. To leave the mansion was enough to keep the minds of the other Smidgens occupied. Things were up in the air. The wisdom of Golly, their mentor and guardian, was held in the highest esteem. Her counsel was being followed. Tight lips were the order of the week.

The upstairs solarium had been checked by Golly for the presence of the mean old tabby and she had declared the area safe. She was close by, checking over the gear and asking in whispers about the care of the moths and the size of the saddle bags.

Fidget kept making faces and rubbing his hands in excited anticipation of the hours just ahead. Fussy was still packing, petting, padding, pampering, perfecting, with intermittent Fussy Flicks, all around her mount. The scene emitted emotional sparks.

On and on went Golly Gee about all the preparations and directions, thought Fidget. With each pressing question, the two Smidgens gave polite and correct answers. "How do you feel? Do you have enough food? Do you have goggles for the moths? The whispering continued, until all was said and affirmed by each of the participants. "Have a safe trip," said Golly, and "be careful".

"At last," said Fidget, under his breath as he strained at being patient and courteous. Golly Gee said a little prayer as they all held hands, and then looking up she wished them both, "Godspeed."

They mounted the awaiting moths that were still adjusting after such a large breakfast of flour and sugar water and the push, pull and poke of four caring hands. All of these gestures would have to last a long time, reasoned their jockeys.

Goggles and mufflers in place, the two little people, with the reins in their hands, gave a tug up and a wave of goodbye. Out the Solarium window they went, with a loving, tearful, Golly Gee looking after them, in the coming dawn. She continued to strain her eyes to follow them up and out over the lawn area until the two small fluttering visions disappeared into an awakening brilliant spring morning. The two adventurers gave a final goodbye wave to Golly Gee and to the Kitchen window where they each were sure Bakka Beans or maybe Redd Peppers would be stationed for a friendly observation.

They then banked around the great lawn and never looked back. Their hearts beat with excitement and pride. They knew that the journey could be so very important and that only they were selected. Each of them drank in deeply of the gentle, invigorating air of the fading night.

The air zephyrs were intermittently mingled with the warm breezes of the new day. The sun's friendly rays began to peek over the distant rolling hills making their way to the ascending Smidgens. They were making progress, emerging above the nearly invisible morning mist rising from the nearby stream.

The constant and harmonious beating of the moth's wings gave out a low humming sound that had the heightening sensation of soaring aloft in an almost mechanical fashion.

When the two were high enough that old Sol's greeting rays, landed warmly on their faces, they signaled each other in a way that showed their joy and triumphs, thumbs up. Far below, the gray tones of the mansion's lawn waiting for the sun's arrival began to show grotesque shadows. Trees, bushes, and other landmarks began to take shape and come to life in the unfolding of the new day. When the Bright Ones glanced at the unfolding of the dawn, lighter and brighter shades of blues, greens, and beige beheld them in its glory. Flying between dark and light, the air began to move in the form of a determined breeze. Each flyer held on tight and guided their mounts to keep flying towards the object of their goal, high up with the greatest visibility of the entire panorama. The wind moved to oppose them, impeding their progress.

Fidget tried to maneuver Swoop in little dives that propelled them forward and then a little to the left. Then he pulled up sharply to the right to gain the advancement needed. It was like sailors expertly using a tacking maneuver.

It was working, but the moths were beginning to show signs of slightly tiring. They hadn't even reached the end of the great lawn area yet. The day was advancing towards a way that springtime always exhibited itself. The warming effect of the sun seemed to slow the breeze a little. The direction of the wind now was changing slightly, and it had a lifting effect.

The land was warming up. This gave them some advantage in their forward progress. With the aviators constant efforts demanding their complete attention it was a startling event when a dark object appeared out of the corner of Fidget's eye.

A pair of black birds had been high up, riding the airwaves, looking for some unsuspecting breakfast repast. The hungry birds were always up early on the air currents so that their appetites could be satisfied with unsuspecting bugs, thereby permitting the rest of the morning to be used for cackling and mischief.

These two birds had left their roosting place before first light and had gained a lot of altitude and attitude. Their attitude was to be avoided. Moths would be tasty breakfast delights. The keen eyesight of the birds became accustomed to the dawn quickly. Looking far below they saw a feisty feline leave the human's house early, to stalk prey in the high grass. A warning for birds that the cat was on the prowl. While scanning the creek area, they noticed movement in the air that piqued their curiosity.

Fidget and Fussy noticed the two birds dropping lower to intercept the little band of moth flyers that took on the appearance of food ascending to the banquet area.

The pair of black birds in precise unison began to close in cunningly on the moths, evaluating the subject's speed, size, and possible retaliation.

Clearly seeing that they were unobserved, the feathered marauders commenced their deadly dive towards the tasty tidbits. With wings tucked back, claws, and beaks at the ready, they cascaded towards their targets at an ever-accelerating speed. Hungry bodies moving like mackerel to the bait; they advanced. Mega mouths, mini minds. Just as conquest and contact were within the grasp of the blackbirds, the meal reacted.

Fidget took his hickory riding staff that Redd had made

and brought it up and down with the speed of lightening to deflect the beak of the first aggressor. Fussy was also able to react with the swiftness needed to accomplish the same effect on the second diver a split second later. The two affected birds continued their downward fall in a most disorganized and painful manner.

"Let's get out of here and hide on the underside of the leaves of that tall oak tree,"

"I am right behind you," blurted Fussy, in agreement.

Fussy and Fidget were more adept than the average tidbits, this morning, it was determined by two discouraged blackbirds.

The two big moths responded to the gentle but authoritative signaling of the reins. They glided down, then up to, and under several large new leaves of the oak. Softly, by nature, they turned over and landed underneath the oak leaves so deftly, it was unnoticeable even to the most discerning eyes. Each Smidgen and moth was perfectly still as their training by the Bright Ones had dictated so many times. The Bright Ones kept a steady hold because of the safety belts they always used keeping them in their respectful saddles.

Swoop and Glide just seemed to know that danger had been narrowly adverted. They, therefore, were holding on tight, with wings slightly folded and eyes closed. Now, all they had to do was to wait for the blackbirds to make some noisy circles and a few inquiring dives in the area. After a short while, the unfed birds would go off in some other direction looking for breakfast from another source.

The Bright Ones were glad when they did. After

all, their adventure had only begun. It was awkward for Fidget to see Fussy. She was also upside down on a nearby leaf. After a time that seemed like an eternity, it was determined that the coast was clear of those raiding birds. Fussy signaled that she was going to guide her mount to the tree trunk, to adjust the sunglasses that the two moths needed in the daytime. Fidget acknowledged and followed her down to the great tree trunk where the necessary maneuver to align the equipment would take place. They landed close enough, and began to speak in whispers.

"That was a close one. I thought that we might have trouble with bats but never the black grackles," whispered Fidget with eyes wide.

"I am glad that Redd made these riding staffs.

"It not only keeps the Moths on course with a gentle touch, but they gave those old bad birds a scare that made them miscalculate their dives," responded Fussy using the staff as a pointer for emphasis.

"Let's get these sun goggles replaced on the Moths and be on our way. We have wasted too much time already and with each hour our task becomes more difficult," Fidget replied. With great urgency each Smidgen went about their duties. Day shades on, straps checked and tightened, knapsack realigned, and reassuring Swoop and Glide that all actions were approved.

Fussy gave the signal that everything was ready and pushed off from the tree trunk and headed skyward towards the woodland canopy.

It had been determined that a flight through the trees that bordered the Rustic Realm's grounds would be more advantageous at this time, because of the impending threat from the skies. Each Smidgen moved their Moth through the highest elevation without sacrificing the trees natural camouflage from higher peering eyes. The trees began to whiz by. The air had lost its crispness of an earlier hour. It seemed so like the many lazy mornings that the Bright Ones had experienced before.

They would hang out one of the upper windows in the Mansion and tell each other stories and adventures of far off places.

Made up stuff about things heard and escapades read. From dreams to hopes to hard work to reality.

Chapter

ELEVEN

*T*hat is what was happening before them. The time moved on easily. Fussy and Fidget seemed to be in a dreamy glide as the Moths took on the near effortless task of flying. Dip and dodge through the forests greenery.

It was like on a roller coaster in a giant salad, brushing near misses of leaf and branch. After a while it was like a spell. So much liberty and ease. Concentration became secondary. They continued on this course until the air turned into a bracing moist elixir bringing them back to reality.

They had reached the rushing stream that flowed in the furthermost reaches of Rustic Realm's manicured lawns. The air rising from all the gurgles and giggles of the stream was cool and moist, even at their higher altitude. An invigorating and welcome change. The pilots turned up the stream, to the right. There was little tree cover here but it didn't seem to matter. The hungry birds had been left far behind. It felt so good to fly low and drink in the streams invisible vapors.

Each dainty waterfall and swell of water was a challenge to the dynamic duo as they moved upstream. Over boulders and around low lying limbs their progress was happily executed. They remembered the map and knew from sightings and stories that when the stream came to a fence, adjacent to a field, they must turn left and follow the fence. The stream meandered to the right and followed the earth's contours upland to its head waters and prolific springs, far away.

With strained vision, they could see a clearing far ahead of them and what appeared to be a wooden fence. Skimming over the creek, it abruptly turned into a wide and serene crystal blue large body of water. Fussy was in the lead on Glide. She is a very good leader when she settles down and gets her priorities organized, thought Fidget. "There is no one else I'd rather be with on this trip than Fussy. She is intelligent and fearless," he concluded with a sigh of contentment.

Fussy was quite low and but now she was gently bringing her Moth up. They had drifted too low. Over this larger body of water, it was imperative that they attain some altitude to avoid any water dangers. Her parents had told her of the dangers about fish near a body of water that would take a Smidgen for tasty bait.

The placid water scene had been like a magnet drawing them both closer to the peaceful silvery surface after so much time over the churning, and agonized bubbling of the earlier trout stream. Looking at the body of water, it appeared as a mirror reflecting the flyers in a way that seemed unreal. It was almost spellbinding. Fidget had stayed a little higher for better observation.

The water between the shore and Fussy began to heave up in a water ball or wave. Through it came the biggest mouth one could imagine. It belonged to the jaws of a great brook trout. It not only opened but also moved in the direction of Fussy and Glide. Fussy pulled hard on the reins to gain a few more inches that are precious. The trout kept coming higher and higher matching her evasive maneuvering, inch for inch. Ultimately, the two looked into each other's eyes.

The trout's eyes, one or each side of its head, seemed to pop and bulge with its straining of movement. Its tail waved in the air, aiding its lunge. The mouth grew larger and wider. The hard teeth-like ridges of the fish were so close that Fussy could almost have touched them. Large cold-water droplets first hit both fliers from the fish's advancement.

Now, with the absolute knowledge that a collision was inevitable Fussy acted with lightening speed. Placing the reins in her mouth she lashed out with her staff with one hand and with the other hand stretched to reach a packet along side her saddle.

Upon obtaining her small treasure, she let it fly right in the mouth of that, out of water, giant trout. It was one of the contributions that Bakka Beans had made. You never know were you might need this and it can be used for so many things, she said when she handed over the packet of minced chili peppers.

The two contestants collided. The mouth miraculously received the scattered hot peppers but not Fussy or Glide. She had slipped out of her saddle on that last reach. Glide had extended his wings to their fullest at the last second and avoiding the waiting mouth. His outstretched wings being greater in size than that hungry trout caused a mishap for the aerial trout. A powerful midair collision sent Glide into slow tailspin, and the trout hurdled back to the cold, deep, dark water below with closed mouth.

Fidget was terrified. Had his eyes deceived him? Were the moth and Smidgen larger that the trout's stomach? Remembering his guardian's counsel at many talks at suppertime, gave Fidget some comfort. *"Are your eyes bigger than your stomach?" Maybe that goes for trout also*, thought the young concerned Smidgen.

The water droplets had reached him along with the sight of horror before his eyes. Swoop was just able to avoid the midair smashup and made a perfect turn to shore. Fidget could only see out of the corner of his eye as his gyration was completed. The final picture his vision gave him was ambiguous. Was she? Did it? His mind conjured up imaginations of all kinds. None good. How would he tell their friends? Was it painful? The adventure is over. What about the fate of Jump Uppity? Even as tears began to burn his eyes he knew that his job was to reach the shoreline, for the search must continue.

With all of his heart and soul, he turned immediately back and looked the situation in the eye. Straining to look back, he jerked the reins of the great moth at the shores edge, and pivoted to see what was the result of that awful second in time. His eyes unfocused because of the well of tears now rising, he turned Swoop to parallel the shore. He heard the plop of the big fish before his eyes cleared to see its splash. "All is lost," thought Fidget as the ripples of the big plunge reached shore.

Chapter
TWELVE

Golly Gee looked out of the windows for her two diminutive friends. She left her frown at the window and returned to the business of running the house. Shortly, she would have to explain the absence of the two Bright One's to the Smidgen Elders. The Bright One's parents had died long ago. Graybub and Oldene always kept close tabs on their charges. Flippant and his friends would positively have something to say. After all, they were left out of the adventure of the decade.

Golly knew that the Uppitys were close to making a decision about selling to anxious buyers. Mr. Snooty had arranged one more meeting with Mr. and Mrs. Pinching. Penelope and Flinch had taken a great liking to the property and had made numerous inquiries to the Uppitys over the last week. Their inquires and contacts seemed to be overbearing and pushy, thought Golly.

"What is all their rush?" muttered Golly as she moved into third gear, remembering today's schedule of cleaning and programming work schedules for the mansion's help.

Redd was sent to the city to pick up the realtor and the two prospective buyers. Pulling into the parking lot of the real estate agent, Redd was impressed with the fact that they all were anxiously awaiting his arrival. The car was gleaming in the spring sunlight as it made its way to the waiting three. They were like three sailors saluting the approaching car. Redd stopped, and opening the door, motioned them to get in the vehicle. One by one, like a giggling gaggle of geese they entered. The level of sounds increased when snickers, guffaws, and chuckles were emitted.

The window between occupants and driver in the big car had a sliding glass panel that was used to permit privacy. Redd therefore closed it, in anticipation of their request. It didn't close perfectly so that their voices began to drift through the minuscule opening from time to time. He was trying to remember the words spoken as he drove the car through city traffic and headed out into the country towards the mansion. He was sure that Golly could help put all of it together to form some sort of tactic that could be used to save Rustic Realm.

Redd glanced at the dashboard clock to see what kind of time frame he had to work with. It would be unlike him to get lost thereby postponing the meeting of the parties by getting lost. No! No one would believe that Redd Peppers ever got lost in this area for any reason. Saying a little prayer under his breath, Redd continued on effortlessly that led to Rustic Realm. He would trust

in the ingenuity of Golly Gee and the grace of God to
take this turn of events and make them right

Chapter
THIRTEEN

*F*idget could finally see clearly as he wiped his eyes one more time. His big moth had instinctively found cover slightly away from the brook's shoreline as the reins had slacked. He became nestled on the leaves of a great overhanging rhododendron, pregnant with blossoms. The pair anxiously searched the panorama for signs of their friends. Swoop began to wave his antennae in an excited fashion, along with puffing sounds in an upstream direction.

After careful scrutiny, Fidget's gaze found Glide, about 50 feet away on the underside of a maple tree leaf. The long forest branch reached into a patch of sunlit tranquility where Glide was carefully drying his wings and recuperating from his recent close call. Fidget continued to hope as he searched again and again the water and shoreline for any evidence of Fussy's possible miraculous escape.

The ripples and movement of the water had all returned to normal and covered the world of danger and struggle that must continue to take place beneath the placid surface.

Fidget came to that place where all logic and teaching began to waver. The words of counsel and advice of Graybub came cascading into Fidget's mind, as he methodically dismounted Swoop. "Do not leave your moth in time of trouble. Do not expose yourself until after long and careful study of the unfamiliar terrain. Be sure no one or nothing sees you!"

"What was that movement in that clump of grass?" Fidget thought out loud as his attention was drawn to the little lush vegetation. The clump had existed in the shallows and had been partly in the water and partly out. It was green with its constant supply of moisture and nutrients.

The grass moved again, but it was out of sync with the more gentle wind that caressed the tops of the luscious vegetation. Wait one more minute, Fidget told himself as he glanced about in all directions and then back to the clump. With his mind and training resisted all the natural impulses to run forward and shout.

He slowly moved in traditional Smidgen style, liquid with no jerks or spastic motions to avoid any enemy's eyes.

Fidget resolved what he must do. Slow and cool like slowly melting ice cream. After all, of the careful procedures that he had been taught, Fidget deftly lowered himself to the forest floor feet first

Fidget continued down the brook's embankment, his thick stick he had found in the brush earlier, at the ready. Closer and closer he nibbled at the distance, carefully reading the occasional uncharacteristic movement of the clump of grass. A frog would be bad. A mink would be bad. Fussy would be good. A crawfish with flashing pinchers devouring prey would be bad. Now at the waters edge, next to the clump, Fidget was able to carefully lean forward using his cudgel as support and commenced to investigate. He parted the grass ever so carefully.

There to his delight was Fussy on her back, looking skyward and gasping for breath. Fidget again surveyed the area on all sides and even in the foliage above them. When all appeared safe and secure, he moved forward and whispered her name close to her ear.

"Fussy, it's me, Fidget. Are you all right?" She promptly turned her head slightly and looked up at Fidget with glazed, reddened eyes. A faint smile crossed her mouth, as she said, "Get me out of here", and then she fainted.

She was soaking wet and exhausted, evidenced by her limp condition like a hankie fresh from the washer. Fidget picked her up by putting one arm under her legs and the other arm around her shoulders Fidget was surprised how easy the lift was.

Fidget with some effort struggled to get Fussy to higher ground. It was a tiring task to climb the bank that contained the forest brook. Fidget was almost sorry that he had decided to keep his pack on.

Fidget was reminded that it was much easier earlier, coming down the slope when mixed with the heat of investigation and anticipation. Peering over the top of the bank, Fidget again looked carefully. Foxes, raccoons, snakes, hawks, and others of that ilk are always to be treated with the greatest respect and given the widest latitude.

All was clear as Fidget made his final lunge to the top with his precious feminine cargo and began to walk towards the tall warm grass in the sunlit opening. Fidget was relieved to see that Glide was still on his leaf, drying his wings and resting. As the two Bright Ones gently settled in the grass, Fussy opened her eyes and began to ask questions about what had happened. Fidget quickly assured her all was copasetic.

Fidget graciously said, "I'll leave some of my extra clothes for you to wear until yours dry out". She changed and dispersed her pack contents in the very warm grasses to dry out as Fidget was returning to Swoop to bring him back to this area.

Fidget moved stealthily out of the tall grass and back to the big leafed plant where Swoop was lingering. Fidget was so relieved that his friend was safe and unharmed.

He had enjoyed rescuing his colleague and almost burst with pride as he had carried her helpless body to safety. She felt lighter and softer than it might have occurred to him in earlier times. He was overwhelmed with a feeling of wanting to protect Fidget from all dangerous outside influences. She was so small and very delicate, more vulnerable than Fidget ever thought before.

He would have to rethink the plan about going to the blue-green- house. It really was never evident to Fidget that Fussy would be in real danger and could be harmed in this adventure. He never saw her as a real girl before.

Fidget raised himself up to the rhododendron leaf where Swoop was patiently waiting. Fidget gently brushed the leading edges of the wings, being careful not to move into the area that was similar to flour dust. After some time, Swoop hummed and puffed for a drop or two of water. Fidget gladly rendered the service. Tightening up the cinch and hopping in the saddle, Fidget adjusted Swoop's goggles for the little flight over to the maple tree.

The pair lifted off of the leaf and flew to the long maple tree limb with its friendly waiting mount. Having safely arrived, Fidget proceeded through the same routine with Glide that he had provided Swoop. He was especially careful to ascertain that the wings of Glide were dry and smooth.

The morning mist was eroding away, and the power of the sun was even more evident than Fidget had noticed earlier. With great care, he continued winding his way through the grasses, initiating only the special whistle to alert Fussy of his approaching presence.

His whistle sounded as though a cricket were chirping. He then cocked his head to hear better with his grand ears to listen for any responses. Only the sound of gently moving fresh spring air came to his attention. Continuing, he skillfully parted the grasses and deftly moved forward until he came upon a scene of special beauty.

There in the middle of the confusion of her pack articles was Fussy, curled up in childlike fashion, asleep. She seemed especially adorable, dressed in his larger sized clothes. Fidget could only hold his breath as he drank in the scene with a certain contentment. Only after the sound of an intruding bee, did the spell break, and Fidget returned to his assigned task of organizing their continuation of the adventure towards the blue green house and its mystery.

"Fussy, Fussy, how do you feel?" he said with certain tenderness as he moved into the scene. He felt a sense of sadness in his waking her up but was compelled to complete their assignment as promised.

"We must plan our schedule and get on with the flight if we are to complete it in one day." He spoke with a sense of authority and kindness. She was opening her eyes and responding to his urging to get up and get ready. All the time she looked like a minuscule doll to Fidget for the first time.

"Yes," she said as she tried to stand on wobbly feet. "We must hurry and pack up and be on our way."

"Not so fast", Fidget interjected as he sat down beside her. "We must take time to talk and reaffirm our plans." She smiled as she sat across from him, "I am so glad you were here when tragedy struck, to save me. I landed in the water after the near mishap and from that height and was dazed. The swim to the clump with full pack and clothes took what was left of my energy and it seemed that I swallowed a lot of water on my way in. I gasped, cried, prayed, and tried to get in the center of that little clump for protection. It seemed like an eternity before you showed up. When you did come to my rescue I just gave up and put myself in your strong, capable hands. I must have passed out." Fussy finished her report, looked up at Fidget, and said, "Thank you".

They seemed to talk for a long time. They began to open up about their hopes and fears. They spoke of the future and common likes and dislikes. "I want to get married and have a family in the traditions of Smidgens in the great out doors. I want to be able to keep up our friendship with Golly Gee and the folks at the Mansion but live the traditional life of our forefathers," said Fussy in almost a whisper "We haven't opened up like this before. I agree with you Fussy said Fidget with conviction in his voice. "I think the time has been well spent, learning more about each other than when we were at home," Fussy said with deep interest. It surely could have gone on for hours, for both of them knew that something wonderful was taking place between them. As precious as the moment was, they also knew that Smidgens lived by rules, duty, discipline, and honor.

Almost at the same instant, they both remembered the trip and its importance. In unison they agreed to pack up and continue. Soon, they were eating the packed food from Bakka's good kitchen and finishing preparations for the climb up the maple limb where their two mounts were waiting.

The interlude was both refreshing and eye opening. Each gently lifted off the maple tree and headed up the valley that the trout stream had made. Taking care to fly high and yet not over the forest's canopy, the Bright Ones headed on their journey, to find Jump or else.

CHAPTER
FOURTEEN

Having arrived at Rustic Realm, Redd pulled up to the front door to let the three excited interlopers exit the big Caddy. Mr. and Mrs. Pinching with Mr. Snooty were all a twitter. They giggled and hissed like serpents closing in on their prey. Mrs. Uppity, who had been signaled electronically, to welcome the guests at the front door with her graceful style.

It all appeared to be a genuine greeting on all sides as they proceeded up the steps and through the great oak doors of the waiting house. Empire Uppity was coming down the hallway to greet his guests. He held in his hand some papers he had just retrieved from his study.

"Welcome to Rustic Realm," said Empire Uppity with an all-inclusive glance at this comical but wily group.

Mater Uppity had taken her customary two steps backwards to allow the group to enter her abode as the group exchanged pleasantries; *it was like a play of puppets*, Mater thought. She also was aware that this episode presented itself as the keystone for the search for her missing son, Jump. *If they buy the place the search for Jump would certainly be diminished*, thought Matter

It is so painful to be so practical, she thought with a certain amount of feminine resentfulness.

Here in her house the negotiations and discussions would have enough room and privacy to conduct the business at hand. Mater said, "may I be excused," and with lowered eyes and shoulders that spoke of the pain and weight of the process before leaving. She would look to the preparations of lunch. Empire had earlier gently released her from her presence at the meeting. Now, he looked at Mater with validating eyes. With an expressive smile, he gently nodded approval at her request and bid the guests to be seated.

Mater left the room and was about to return to the kitchen when Golly Gee approached her. Golly Gee, knowing the significance and gravity of the meeting decided to speak up.

"Mater, may I have a word with you?" Golly Gee used only the mistress of the house's first name when alone or when a few close friends were present. Mater knew immediately that it was the request of a friend and important.

"Yes," she said, as she motioned for them both to retreat into the sanctum of a small study just off the paneled hallway.

Mater invited Golly to sit in one of the lavish chairs with a motion of her hand as she slowly sat in the one opposite it.

Both women were intensely attentive. Golly Gee was the first to begin to speak.

She prefaced her remarks by informing Mater that lunch would be ready in a few minutes. It was a courteous practice and good manners.

"Mater, you shouldn't sell the house at this time," Golly blurted out in stilted words. These words hung heavy in the air of the chestnut and black walnut room. The words were out of character. They were said in such a way that it was hard to tell their emotional origins or weight.

Command? Request? Inquiry? Friend? Adversary? The seconds were being ticked off by the grandfather clock in the corner. It was so quiet that even their breathing sounds invaded the sanctity of the moment.

With great dignity Mater glanced down at her stylish dress, carefully brushing away an uninvited fold or imaginary lint particle. Pausing to clearly understand the moment, she breathed deeply. Mater eventually looked up and broke the silence with only one word.

"Why?" Mater looked down at her lap and smoothed her dress once again in a time-honored motion that was characteristic of her when she was patiently awaiting the passing of difficult times.

Golly Gee replied, "I have worked for you and Mr. Uppity for some time and have enjoyed it and our special relationship. When I came to Rustic Realm, I just knew that this house and land were different than any other place I had ever worked. It was in part because of the size and location of the mansion as well as the people like you and Mr. Uppity, and eventually Jump.

It wasn't too long before I noticed as I worked and

sang for joy throughout the house that out of the corner of my eye I noticed movement. When I looked quickly there was apparently nothing there. When I talked about it to Bakka and Redd, they also confided that they also had noticed images and movement out of the corners of their eyes. We determined eventually that when we were happy and joyous the incidences increased. We devised a plan to have Bakka sing and dance in the kitchen while I peeked out from the large broom closet for any movement. When we executed the plan, much to my surprise, I could see several tiny forms coming out from the shadows. Pixie-like, they danced and mimicked the exuberant Bakka, behind her back and just out of her sight. When they came closer to the broom closet door, I could see they were a small assembly of jubilant miniature folk. In sheer elation, I opened the door, reached out, and grabbed one of them. The balance of the miniature throng scattered and disappeared in a twinkling of an eye. Fortunately the one I caught was the grand patriarch of the wee band. His name is Graybub." Mater gently interrupted, as her eyes had grown to about exploding size.

"I think I've seen them too," Mater related excitedly, as she moved forward to the edge of her chair. "When Jump first came to live with us, I was so happy that I sometimes cried. I thought the movements that I noticed were just the blurring of the tears of joy. Many times, I felt surrounded with corporate joy and the presence of affection.

Jump and I would read books and talk together about so many things. Sometimes we would just giggle for the fun of it. When Jump and I were laughing we would notice the little darting movements. Jump would say they were little people, but I told him it was just a figment of his active imagination.

The long adoption process was both painful and emotional for us all, and I thought maybe he was saying this to share his joy with imaginative others. I didn't give it much thought because all I cared about was Jump and the gratitude in my heart for having him as our son."

Mater gave out a deep sigh as the loss of her adoptive son Jump, and of the happy times. The melancholy washed over her countenance like a cold blue fog as she contracted back in her chair.

Golly Gee continued with her narrative after a few seconds that were given to Mater to reflect on the mental joyous scenes in her mind.

"Graybub began to sputter and rant while I held him in my hand. His gray beard flapping in the air. He scolded me for being so nosy," Golly Gee continued

"Bakka was in his face and began to scold him in her direct way. I held on until he calmed down and eventually repented of his rash behavior. Thereafter, he was telling us everything about the bevy of his bantam breed. As he revealed and blathered as most politicians do, his little companions began to reappear. Ultimately we became, one big happy family.

While all of this was transpiring, Redd Peppers had observed all at a window from outside. After a few brief explanations to the little people, I finally let Redd into the kitchen.

We three apparently were the only ones to know of their existence here at Rustic Realm. I am certain that

Jump also knows about their existence. He is so clever and perceptive.

They are called Smidgens. They know of Jump's kidnapping and have tried to assist by listening to all the events at the mansion. They are quite adept at flying on the backs of some giant moths, from time to time."

Golly noticed as she took a deep breath with her extensive narrative that Mater was becoming more interested with every sentence. She also was certain that Mater didn't think she was crazy. Mater had slowly moved forward again in her chair. New life was beginning to radiate and sparkle from her eyes.

The deep set lines about her mouth that had been turned down for so many months, now at least appeared to be on a new horizontal trend. *Mater seemed to sense that something positive was going to be about Jump and his situation,*' thought Golly. She would have to be careful not to disappoint her listener or to simplify the ramifications of the events yet to be told.

Golly cleared her throat and continued, "I have made very good friends of these little people. They have an insatiable appetite for curiosity. They have recently noticed something curious on one of their special flights in the great outdoors on the backs of the mammoth moths they have befriended. Two of these young Smidgens have spied out a dark blue-green house inside the great woods, not easily visible from the air or road, apparently. It is some how camouflaged for deceptive activities. The two Smidgens barely noticed a wisp of smoke rising from the chimney on their recent flight, indicating habitation. They wanted to return immediately after that sighting. All of us thought that the area had been searched for Jump and yet no mention was made of the presence of this little house. We soon concluded that it was overlooked because of faulty or incomplete information. No one knows of its existence."

"Yes, yes," said Mater in controlled revitalized excitement. Her eyes quite wide and shining with renewal. "I remember now when we had the meeting on the patio when I noticed you at the door. The men were talking about a parcel of land that was sold long ago without the proper record. Mr. Uppity and I didn't think too much about it but had wondered why it was sold. In addition, what had happened to that little piece of land since that time? When Mr. Snooty, the realtor, informed the group that a curious couple from Strangeville had purchased the property, a cold chill went through my heart."

Mater seemed to shiver as she relived that moment of revelation. "I just knew that event had something to do with Jump's disappearance. What can we and the Smidgens do now to see if this blue-green painted house has some relevance in our quest for Jump's return?" Mater looked at Golly with breathless anticipation as her maternal instincts rose in expectation with her new hope.

"Two bright young Smidgens are at this very moment on an excursion to the house in question. We are awaiting their return home to inform us of their findings. If there is some substance of hope in those results, we would not want the Rustic Realm sold. Redd Pepper's and Bakka's detailed observations seemed to coincide with my hunches about them. Our desire is to have you stall the negotiations or transaction until this report is in our possession to evaluate. We would keep you constantly informed and solicit your counsel on any new proceedings."

Golly, Gee sat back a little in her chair with a look of relief because she had finally unburdened herself to her mistress.

"I will do just that. I'll stall the sale with tact and finesse" said Mater as she arose from her sitting position and exited the room with a new air of confidence and faith.

Chapter

FIFTEEN

*L*ooking up the small valley, Fidget could see that the trout stream would soon break out into a large, flat meadow. There would be no safety cover for the little band of fliers when they reached that point.

Fidget remembered that earlier in the planning stage that they had to turn left 90 degrees left and follow the fencerow that marched up and out of the stream's valley to the place that was on the edge of the great woods. He was sure now they would be able to locate the little blue-green-green-green house that was just inside the woodsy boundary. Fidget motioned to Fussy with hand signals that they would soon turn left and precede in an upland direction. Fussy quickly signaled with hand and face gestures that she understood and added that she wanted to go first to lead the way.

Fidget acknowledged and began to pull the rein on his giant shuttle to slow him down, so Fussy could pass as they made the grand arc towards the target of their endeavors. The transition was made flawlessly, and Fussy was heading lower to take advantage of the vegetation growing along the fencerow. The great woods became increasingly denser at their ascending out of the little valley. It was a much longer way than it appeared to them in their earlier flight. Greater skill was now exercised as the unevenness of the scrub trees and bushes made for a roller coaster ride. A cool breeze from the deep forest could be felt occasionally, whispering its message of a spring day on the wane. The beautiful sun was in its descending mode with clouds gathering on the horizon. Gray seemed to permeate the western skyline to their right and prompted each Smidgen to remember an old proverb, about a red sky. *(Red sunset tonight, tomorrow is sailors delight.)* What about a gray sky?

They were cresting the imposing foot hill beneath them. They would have to chance higher air for a more revealing look. Each gave the okay sign and began to urge their mounts to circle in an aggressive upward spiral. The strong moths began to catch the breezes and were power lifted heavenwards. It was a dizzy ordeal as blood pounding exhilaration fused with the giddy upward rotations continued.

Fidget and his mount, Swoop, attained a very high vantage point when Fidget noticed something unusual. It was a blue-green house, located just a few hundred yards into the forest on the back slope of a small knoll. Hard to notice at this angle of observation because of the weather wearied wooden, shingled roof that blended with the surrounding woods, camouflaging its existence.

The tiny clearing was barely enough for the dwelling, but it was now in plain view. Fussy saw it about the same time and pointed in that direction. Fussy pointed over, and again as she bent forward in her saddle on the rotation that took her closest to the object of her excitement. A big smile flashed across her face in triumph. Fidget finally got her attention and signaled for them to dive now that they had their bearings. This time they modified the moths upward achievements and would rush earthward and into the woods to their objective, the blue-green house.

The daring dash downward was filled with rushing air. Fussy's glistening hair waved frantically. Her shiny locks were emerging from beneath her flight cap and extending into the wind. It reminded Fidget of Mater Uppity's beautiful lace curtains dancing in a summer breeze.

A thing of beauty, thought Fidget as he followed Fussy's tight pull-up and entry into the forest. After such a rapid descent, it almost felt like slow motion as they now fluttered and flew past the great trees. The air was calm and cool. Moisture from the forest floor rose up to the flying foursome and made the atmosphere feel heavy. The canopy of new leaves on the trees became higher and tighter as they moved forward in the direction of the petite house.

Not too high and not too low was the plan as they moved past the stately oaks, shagbark hickory, mighty maples, handsome eastern cedars, poplars, and occasionally an American Holly were now their companions. A few pine trees were seen up ahead. Most likely to deny any inquiring eyes of discovery. Suddenly, there it was just before them, the object of their long and intense mission. Gently directing the mounts to keep in the limbs of the lofty hardwood trees the two Smidgens softly landed, high up in tallest of the wooden sentinels. From here they could rest and observe any activity in and around the dwelling below.

They whispered congratulations with smiles .A fresh breeze caught them full in the face, and all at once they both realized how late in the day it was getting, and that the weather was beginning to change into threatening stormy indication. They, by mutual agreement, moved the group to a fungus bump on the tree trunk for greater stability. They also resigned themselves to the one thing they had promised Golly Gee not to do if possible. They would have to stay the night because it was too late to try to return to the great mansion.

"I pray that Golly understands that these circumstances demand unusual decisions," whispered Fussy as she began to unpack a few things for the stay and search ahead of them.

"Can't be helped," said Fidget as he joined her in the quiet assembling of gear for the hours to come.

"My hope is that they are all aware of our maturity and the importance of this assignment," he added with a touch of satisfaction in his voice. They were sitting cross-legged, opposite each other, discussing the various ways to gather the information about, whom, what, and why. "If we see no one in the day light we can take off the moths sun shades and fly down to the windows for a better look," opined Fidget.

"It will be dark soon, and we will need that cover to get closer to the house for close up views of the occupants and activities," said Fussy in perfect agreement. They continued to discuss the situation and set about preparing the few things they would need in the investigation. A quick snack was also prepared with busy fingers and admiring looks. Bread and Cheese were served along with fruit juice to nourish the little crew. The moths were also fed, and a time for rest was set aside. It appeared that the moths were nervous, but upon closer examination it was discovered that the tree sap on the broad branch that they were perched on was posing a sticky problem for them. They moved to safer quarters.

Since all below was silent and with no apparent movement the little band soon nestled back for a nap. The light faded with the approaching night. It reminded Fidget of the time he went down into a well, and the only light was directly above. The moon, now overhead, agonized in its attempt to send beams through the now gathering leaden skies. *The night began to feel smothering thought,* Fussy as her eyes closed in that moment before sleep transports its subject away to the land of nod.

Bang! The report came to the two siesta seekers simultaneously. "It sounded like a shot," said Fidget, as he raised up from the pine bough. Fussy replied, whispering in her sleepy voice. "It came from down below, near the house." They now both crawled along the branch to its outer edge for a better look. Each took a deep breath of discovery as their eyes grew wide and round. They turned to look at each other for a second and then returned their gaze to the object of their amazement. Far below was the top of a tousled blond towhead. The faint light coming from the house and the periodic peek of the moon revealed the form of a small boy. His features were frail and gaunt. His clothes were scruffy and unkempt. His body sagged forward as though under a heavy burden.

Could this be Jump Uppity? Fussy whispered into the night.

He took a few small steps forward, towards the woods, as though calculated to evoke a response. It did.

"Don't be going too far now!" Came a crude voice from within the house. "You don't want me to send old Rattler, our eager dog, to fetch ye back, do ye?" The voice was course but definitely a woman. The pitiful figure far below slowly turned and retreated to the house and reentered through the old screen door. This time when it closed, it was neither as startling nor as loud as when the Smidgens first heard it.

CHAPTER
SIXTEEN

ld Rattler looked up from his warm bed in the corner by the great stove and purposely showed his canine teeth, accompanied by a throaty snarl for effect when the young boy reentered the room. It was his thing. Rattler was programmed by the gruff voice of his nasty mistress.

"Good boy," came the old dry gravelly voice.

Nastine Gruffly sat down at her small, cluttered desk. Casting one final glance at Jump where he sat like a fragile doll, in the furthermost corner in a small, battered straight-backed chair. Efficiently Nastine returned to her accounts and ledgers.

Nastine was not as old as she looked. Her hair was gray and resembled a number 3 steel wool pad. The brow of her forehead was deep with furrowed lines. Her skin was dry and in the subdued light of the room emerged as unpolished silver.

She always moved in a manner that suggested that she had roving pain in her body, just as though the splinters of life were everywhere and never removed. Her face looked though she had just finished tasting some battery acid. On every finger rested a beautiful, brilliant ring. Diamonds, rubies, sapphires, emeralds, all set in gold, silver, and platinum. Dilated pupils now were squinting and straining in the delightful process of bookkeeping.

Jump sat in his chair. The evening meal of boiled potatoes and cabbage soup was long over. The pots and pans were washed and dried and had been put a way. The utensils of the day, including the flasks and beakers used for the chemical and designer drug making had been cleaned and returned to their shelves and cabinets. The chemicals needed for making illegal drugs had been lined up in alphabetical order, waiting for the next usage. The little kitchen had been tidied, and all that was left to do was to sit in the corner until Jump's eyes became heavy with sleep. Nastine then would notice and order Jump to go to bed.

It was a scene played out for almost a year now. Ever since she and her husband, Bark, kidnapped the little boy near his home, they had kept him busy doing all the hard and dirty jobs of a slave in a sweatshop. More of an asset than a ransom, Nastine had surmised, and practical.

Jump sat still with his little, bony hands folded as the hope of that day was fading and evaporating with the second closing of the back screen door. Sighs too deep to calculate from where they originated, came from the little chest as the gloom of despair again settled in the aching heart of Jump.

Nastine's eyes lazily glanced to Jump's corner of the

room and then returned to figures and sums before her. She was committed to conclude the task of bookkeeping of their little illegal business before her husband returned. She relished the thought of her being the el supremo of decadence. The lives she affected by her concocted plethora of drugs gave her a sense of power that fed her black and evil heart. It had been a lot of risk to rise to such ignoble heights; she pondered with a cloak of self pity. Even so, she continued to daydream about the future events in their lives. "The Riviera would be nice," she muttered with envy under her breath

Bark had gone to town to complete one of their transactions and return with new information about the sale of the adjoining property.

Bark had told her earlier, Some big time city slicker named Pinching wants to buy the Old Rustic Realm Estate. If he could buy it, then they promised to include the little blue-green- house and our business. This would make for a complete and lucrative drug-manufacturing site. Far away from everything and out of the reach of prying eyes.

With the land purchase, Pinching could expand the operation to fit the needs of the suckers that used these illegal and illicit drugs that we make, thought Nastine out loud as the sound of their little pickup could be heard chugging up the last 100 feet to the house.

Another vehicle was right behind Bark. *It sounded much quieter and appeared to be one of those four wheel drive vehicles*, thought Nastine as she leaned precariously back on her chair to catch a glimpse through the living room window of the new arrival. She heard one clunking door slam and then another subtler slam from the vehicles.

Bark has brought someone to have a meeting about the sale, supposed Nastine, as she got up and grabbed Jump. "In yer room," she growled. Nastine opened an old closet door, and Jump was hurriedly pushed, in and the door quickly closed behind. The chilling sound of cold steel against cold steel was heard, as the recently attached bolt was slammed shut that isolated little Jump from the rest of the world.

Jump landed on his cot. It took up all the space of the closet except for six inches all along its length.

This gave him just enough room to sit on the cot and dangle his skinny little legs over its sides. The closet was stuffy because there were no windows. A small brave band of light entered under the door giving Jump an outline of his tattered shoes. An arrow of light came into the closet via the keyhole that Jump sometimes played with, pretending he could become small enough to ride out through its opening on the beam of light. He had spent many evenings in here as Bark and Nastine participated in clandestine meetings with crooks and drug pushers.

Some nights it would be just the two of them with bottled booze, stumbling bodies, incoherent laughter, and babbling. Jump was always afraid and prayed that he wouldn't be hurt. Usually, he would lie on his cot and pull up the covers and try to shut out all the confusion.

Many times he put his ear up to the door and listened to what was being said hoping for some conversation that would be about him and his possible release. The house was small, and he could make out most of the sounds of voices and what they meant as they moved through the tiny rooms.

"Nastine, Mr. Pinching would like a drink," snapped

Bark. He said with rancor in his snarl. "Have you finished all the bookkeeping?" Jump could hear his big boots come into the kitchen for a look-see about the bookkeeping. "Where's the brat?" He barked as he turned back to the front room.

"In bed, where do you think he is in this match box of a house?" She said nastily.

She proceeded in getting Mr. Pinching his drink. "Here is your drink, sir," she said as honey dripped from her highly pitched voice. Bark grabbed the bottle and then all of them sat down in the front room.

"Git me another bottle," he said as his big frame plopped in the giant, torn, artificial leather recliner chair making its usual almost vulgar sound of escaping air. After a few more grunts and oaths their voices lowered, and it became more difficult to make out the complete sentences of the conversation. Bark's voice began to slur.

It was difficult for Jump to hear, but some words came through, and when put together, he was able to assemble some information. Words, like "sale" and "drugs" and "old man Uppity" all began to make sense. "Old woman," must mean Mater he thought. His heart was touched anew as he remembered his new Mom and the great days at Rustic Realm. Something big was happening. It was not the same old humdrum that was his ear's diet for so many months.

Words began to tumble into the closets that were hard to place. "Fly in the ointment, old biddy," and "cold water", came through.

As the evening wore on, someone got up and moved

about. Jump took a seldom-used painful position to see through the keyhole.

Wiggling down in front of the door and pulling up the cot partway with his back until it tilted he prepared for his observations. This allowed him enough room to crouch down to look through the little opening. Turning his face sideways, he was able to place his right eye at the keyhole opening and see into the kitchen that was still faintly lit. Slowly, he looked in all directions until he spotted Bark at a little table, with a bottle under his arm and some papers in his hand.

Soon, Bark returned to the front room. "Here are the most recent figures for our operation. These should convince all concerned that the price is well below what could be made here if a bigger concern would run it." Bark poured himself another drink as he unceremoniously handed over the papers to Mr. Pinching and plopped down in his big torn puffy chair. Nastine sat opposite Mr. Pinching on an old bedraggled couch.

Jump was now alternating with his ear and then his eye to the keyhole to efficiently gather information.

"Jump could hear Mr. Pinching speaking with his high pitched voice. " As I told you, the deal didn't go through today as we first thought it would. At the last minute, these changes came not because of money but because of the request of the lady of the household. I am sure we can finish up in a few days and seal the contracts. Then we will buy this place, and you two can go off and retire in the sunny South."

"It better go through" burped brusque Bark.

He sat there with his big bushy head sunk into his chest. His eyes were deep set and looked like burned out charcoal. They had difficulty seeing through thick round glasses and then past his nose. His hands were big and his nails unclean. His breath spoke of beer. Old Rattler whined at his feet, occasionally looking up for an anticipated pat on his shaggy head.

Their business finally concluded, Nastine and Pinching arose and prepared for goodbyes. Nastine continued to echo her husbands concerns and declarations in that high pitched, honey clad voice she reserved for such occasions. "It had better go through. I have worked hard to make this part of the organization very profitable. We are surely pleased with all the work you have done to get this sale on the right track."

Bark grunted some parting words. "See ya later, old Pinch", as he unsuccessfully tried to gain footing and stand in an upright position.

Jump figured that Pinching probably left with a meager smile and a halfhearted wave of the hand since time with the Grufflys evoked glad gestures when leaving their presence.

Jump could see and hear the Grufflys with his young eyes and ears. Nastine returned from the front stoop and closed the door. She stood before Bark and his glazed eyes and began to systematically build a tirade that was so common that each just played their part. One with Nastine's mouth babbling and Bark with glazed over eyes.

In the lull, Jump glanced about the kitchen pensively, one last time and noticed a blurred movement just outside the window. Something faintly outlined by the meager available light was a flutter. *Just a moth*, he thought as he righted his cot and lay down. Memories inundated his mind, and tears welled up in his eyes. *Will this ugliness never end?* The sandman finally found the little imprisoned boy to take him to better places.

Chapter

SEVENTEEN

Mater Uppity went down the hallway to the library, to attend another meeting she knew would still be in progress. Her steps were bouncy and purposeful. She hesitated at the great library doorway and drew deep in her lungs the air of expectation mingled with determination. Pivoting on her left foot she flowed into the library with uplifted arms and an inquiring voice.

"Who is ready for a wonderful lunch? Oh, you will love what cook has prepared. Tasty little sandwiches, salad with tangy dressings, zippy beverages that will tickle your nose and deserts that one would die for."

Her husband had stopped in mid-sentence to witness his fluttering wife with wide eyes and slack jaw amazement. She moved about the room, chirping away at the guests about the waiting delights. One by one, the guests, each in turn looked up from important documents to witness this effervescent, efficacious, effeminacy. In a moment or two, she had convinced them that this repast was far more important than any old tasteless business. Slowly but surely, each rose from their sitting positions to follow Mater Uppity and her sparks of tenacity concerning her visions of culinary pleasures.

Her husband's neat mustache quivered nervously, not knowing where this explosive package of energy had emanated. The little troupe partly marched and partly shuffled out of the library and into the hallway. The conversation turned to the weather and drifted slowly to comments on the beauty of the house.

'I can see that the mansion and its setting has tonic and joy for Mrs. Uppity, said Mrs. Pinching with an eye towards the revived and vibrant Mater Uppity.

Mr. Pinching also gave a comment of hope and observation.

"Mater, I can tell that you have been thinking about selling with a renewed joy and conviction."

Leading the group and listening attentively, Mater WAS a revived and renewed lady. It appeared to Mater that she could see clearly for the first time in a long span. The dreary fog of despair had lifted, and a new vista had opened up for her. JUMP COULD BE FOUND BY THE LITTLE SMIDGENS WHEN OTHERS HAD FAILED

She could see into these people who were strangers in her house. It wasn't pretty. They had ulterior motives and a penchant to be overly desirous to buy the mansion and its properties. All her guests' demeanors radiated distrust and wariness by their shifting eyes, nervous comments and forced smiles.

Time, distance, and effort were no longer barriers. She felt like a tigress with all her instincts intact, and working with a sense that her child was to be found. No one or no thing would get in her way now that the scent of hope had surfaced and presented itself.

Mater continued to lead the little gaggle to the end of the hallway and through the French doors that led to the back patio.

Bakka Beans had just finished the place settings on the table and presently would blend into the background until Mater had seen that all was in order.

"The food will be excellent as we gave one of the finest cooks in the area. She can take something simple and create a masterpiece of appealing cuisine." Mater finished her dialogue and now nodded for each to sit at an appointed place.

During these few seconds, Mater also glanced about with her bright sparkling gray eyes with the most expressive smiles. She finally gave Bakka the sign of approval by a nod of her head, capped it off with a faint wink.

As the little group began to consume the splendid lunch, Mater began her businesslike discourse. "My, my, my," she said. "How could we ever consider to move without taking some of our special roses? Moreover, there are several small statues in the formal gardens that we had purchased in Italy that I can't part with, ever. I have also been thinking that we might have a small parcel of land deeded to us for our retirement years.

"Yes, oh my yes, there is so much yet to determine the

many details of the sale of Rustic Realm that it will take days to have all the new papers drawn up and properly executed, said Mater."

Mater dipped a celery stick into some special -green dip and crunched down with a loud sound as she simultaneously glanced up and into the eyes of her guests. The guests' eyes had become glassy, and their mouths seemed to be more open than closed as the weight of what Mater had disclosed became crystal clear. Each one drank often. Scheming mouths tended to dry out quickly.

Mater turned her head slowly toward the realtor and slowly addressed him as he painfully tried to gulp some improperly chewed food.

"Mr. Snooty, what can you tell us about the parcel of land that was partitioned and sold just before Mr. Uppity and I purchased Rustic Realm. Who bought it and what has been done, if anything with the property?"

Mr. Snooty swallowed hard and opened his mouth but nothing came out except, "uh."

Mater vaulted into the split second silence.

Three mouths had tried to open and utter something in causal, soothing response. Snooty, Mr., and Mrs. Pinching tried with slack jaw to utter someking of lie but without success. Too late! Mater, the Tigress, had pounced into the fray without fear or trembling. "Come now Mr. Snooty, something must have been done with that little piece of land."

"A pond built, a retreat or camp or even a cabin for weekenders. Surely, you would know, sir." Mater coyly looked at her husband and then smoothed out an imperceptible wrinkle in her dress as she waited for a response.

Mr. Snooty was sputtering and Mr. and Mrs. Pinching were coughing as the moment hung heavily with apprehension and hesitation. They all three began to speak at once and only Mr. Snooty prevailed as the Pinchings faded. Mr. Snooty broke into a strained moment of silence with a dry prevaricating retort.

"Uh, so many things have happened since those days, so I don't pretend to know all that goes on. I'll have to question my subordinates for details if they are available. I can see that we need to assemble new papers immediately for the agreements so that we can accommodate all of your requests.Mr.Snooty said."

His great bushy eyebrows seemed to blend above his nose as two beady eyes below them darted about serpentine-like at the faces of his assembled two ne'er-do-wells. Trying so hard to evaluate all of the countenances, he held up his scrawny hand and stretched out his concluding, connecting, and controlling word, saying, "Soooooo, we must finish here and depart right away so that not a minute is lost in the orchestration of all the details and the wishes of all parties."

"My people will be in touch with your people, and we hope that all can be accomplished in a few days."

He stood up and held the back of Mrs. Pinching chair, who was fair ready to explode with unspoken comments and observations. Her red face met the purple rage of her husband, because of all the complications and staling, but neither spoke a word that might reveal the real intent for buying the mansion, which was for drug trafficking.

"Have your man meet us at the front door, and we will be off to initiate these matters right away."

The realtor remained in apparent control of himself by not speaking to reveal his anger at these complications, as he slowly headed towards the front of the house.

"Come, come, we must let Mr. and Mrs. Uppity formulate all of their requests that will be required for the sale so that their people can contact our people for the final closings, squeaked Mr. Snooty to the two Pinchings."

Empire Uppity had called on the intercom for Redd Peppers to come at once to the great front entrance. Empire followed the accelerated moving little band down the great hall to the front door.

In the front of the troupe was the still mumbling Mr. Snooty with his great eyebrows moving up and down. His scrawny neck moved in unison with his bobbing head as he half sprinted, half walked, down the hall. His beady eyes darted to and fro, as he hungrily saw the beautiful paintings, vases, and hand carved woodwork in the hall. Tapestries hung strategically above the parquet floor. He desired things as well as orchestrating malevolent enterprises. Red Face and Purple Puss Pinchings followed this black hearted realtor

Both Pinchings were in a blue- funk. They realized they would have to wait awhile to get this house and land for their illicit enterprising, detestable, caper.

Off in a quiet corner the tigress eyed the retreating goats. *Tried to trap the unsuspecting*, she thought. Out loud in the electrified air she said quietly, "Now we will have time to snare these terrible people and see whether they can lead us to some difficult answers."

As she observed the departing wretched protoplasm, Golly Gee joined her in the subdued light. "I see that by the remaining food the little gathering broke up early. If you want to, I can clean up or leave some for the two of you."

Mater slowly turned as the retreating refuse was carted off in the big caddy and responded with a know-all smile.

"Leave enough for Empire and myself. I am famished, and we have much to discuss now that I feel what I feel and see what I see. Keep me posted of any new developments," she said as she walked to her returning Husband. Golly Gee went to the lanai to clear three places and tidy up two places. As she exited she could hear the strong voice of Mater. "Come, Empire we have much to talk about."

Chapter

EIGHTEEN

The two Smidgens were thrilled as they looked down from their high perch. They looked at each other and exchanged wide eyed agreement that they had found Jump alive.

"That was Jump down there," Fidget said as he rubbed his eyes to be certain that what he had seen was real. Fussy began to crawl back to the tree trunk and the company of the moths as she quietly replied," he looked terrible. We will have to execute a plan as soon as possible to try to rescue him without going all the way back to the mansion.

As they reached the great tree's center and the close proximity of their moths they slowly calmed their own excitement by taking deep breaths. They were glad they had paid attention to Graybub and Oldene's lessons on self control and proper conduct in emotional situations.

"Take deep breaths and count to a favorite number.

"Don't say anything for a moment or two until your total self has digested the circumstances. Say a little prayer for help."

They each raised their heads and looked at each other and flashed faint but knowing smiles that reached deep inside to confirm their profound friendship. Fidget spoke first.

"We must fly the moths down and see more of the surroundings and every thing about the house. We must ascertain which room he is in and if he is hampered or restricted in any way. A warm spring evening might find a window open. We can free him; I am sure, even if we are little."

Fussy leaned over and kissed Fidget as he lowered his head in verbal depletion. "Of course we are little. Of course, we are going to free him. We will find a way even if the task looks too difficult. Quitters quit, but winners don't. That must be our motto. Let's get the moths ready and pack up. Then we can begin to reconnoiter while the moon is still peaking in and out of the clouds. Jump will be home before you know it."

Fussy took Fidget's hand. Now, they were both involved in the task of readying the moths for their night time flight. Grooming their wings, and finishing feeding them, they took a few drops of water to each moth. Saddles were set, and packs securely loaded.

From time to time each would glance at the window of what apparently was the kitchen. Faint light still permeated the dark back yard. Silence pervaded the house like a tomb. Just when all of their preparations had been completed a far away sound located the sensitive pointed ears of the two Smidgens.

Two motor vehicles were slowly approaching the little clearing from the bowels of the great woods. They appeared suddenly out of the dense vegetation with four headlights that played crazily through the night sky as they came over a little hill and one stopped at the house. The old pickup parked under the carport. Lights out. The driver's door of the stubby piece of transportation opened, and a figure eased out into the now moonlit yard.

The other vehicle was a four wheeled vehicle, a newer kind and much quieter. The driver of the four-wheeler seemed to move like an eel. He slid out of the machine and oozed across the few feet of yard and writhed up the steps of the house behind the other, larger figure.

The pick up truck driver walked liked a bear and mounted the stairs in loud thumps. They disappeared from the Smidgens line of sight as they entered the Blue-green house. Verbal commands and comments emitted in barks, similarly to a disgruntled sergeant's, voice.

The door opened on the other side of the house from the kitchen, underneath the porch, and was verified by a momentary stream of yellow light flashing in the yard.

Without a word the two little troopers moved back to their respective moths and mounted. With hand signals they agreed to take flight and circle the house for an overall view and then lower to one of the windows for a close up appraisal of the situation.

The great moths wings began to reach into the warm night air in silent and yet powerful strokes of advancing movements. All four participants were quickly ascending higher up and then began to methodically circle the dwelling below.

The moon continued to sporadically appear and disappear at the whim of the passing clouds. A kitchen, with eating area, a living room, and one bedroom.

Fidget motioned to Fussy about the large cloud soon to obscure the moon and that they should now go down for a closer look. Like a great hand coming over a projection lamp the night suddenly became dark.

Waiting a few seconds for their eyes to become accustomed to the gloomy scene below they nudged their flying mounts to descend.

Ultimately, they glided around the house and slowly past the windows for a more detailed view of their target.

Flying past what must have been the bedroom, now clothed in darkness the moved slowly around to the front and a larger window with torn curtains hopelessly trying to conceal the clandestine meeting within.

Fidget could see all three actors on stage and turned about for a second view to remember more details. They spied a skinny man with beady eyes, a barking bear, and a silvery rumpled crone sat in the tiny living room, discussing things.

On they flew to the back of the house and the window near the back door. It was a kitchen of severe proportions with a desk and table. Here also was the big iron stove, cupboards, and a pantry door. The window was pushed up to allow air in for the stove and for cooling the kitchen. They both spotted the Achilles heel simultaneously and pointed to it in unison. They were now moving and thinking almost as one, as hand signals indicated a spiral upward and a landing on the roof above, the answer to their prayers.

The roof was rough, enabling the moths a landing and an anchor. The two travelers dismounted gingerly and set about to unpack some rope to make a descent down to the window for further investigation.

They attached the rope to one of the gutter supports and cast the rope over the side and fed it down to the window ledge.

Fussy had already begun to descend the secured rope as Fidget came to the gutter for any help that might be needed. None required. He also began the repelling process to reach the windowsill.

Ensconced on the windowsill, they looked into a darkened room that reeked of a legion of odors many of which were unknown to the Smidgens. Burnt sugar and paint thinner were the most prevalent. Each moved to one side of the window casing and could see all the way into the living room.

They heard the voices very distinctly now.

"The old lady of the mansion, I think was becoming suspicious of our motives. She and her husband appeared to want to back out of the sale." Talk of Mater and the sale of the mansion floated out the window. The sale that the thin man had hoped for should have taken place this afternoon had failed because of Mater Uppity's insistence upon certain changes. The big bear of a man came into the kitchen suddenly, and went to the little desk for some papers. The two Smidgens had seen him coming and had pressed themselves tightly against the side window's casing. They prayed that he did not come to shut the window or notice the little rope still hanging down from the gutter brace.

Bark rummaged about the desk and soon returned to the living room with grunts of information for the thin man. "I have the original papers for the sale of this property. Maybe it would help us."

The benevolent spies waited patiently as the three occupants continued their discussion. In the front room, as seen by the Smidgens through the open kitchen door the saw the thin man get up and was ushered out the front door and where he drove off into the forest's gloom. The two remaining players began to exchange verbal abuses. "I told you this project would fail because of the inept Pinching involved. Don't you remember the fuss he made when buying this out of the way property?" Nastine was getting madder by the moment of the near failed purchase of Rustic Realm.

"Oh. Just shut your tater trap and quit fussing all the time," said Bark Gruffly.

Fidget saw it as an opportunity to get a much-needed tool from the kit he had left with his moth, Swoop. With a high pitched whistle that humans could not hear and two tugs of the dangling rope he sent a signal to swoop to make a slow pass by the window. Presently his mount was hovering close by and passed in such a manner that Fidget could reach out and secure his tool kit, and then Swoop returned to the roof as ordered by hand gestures by Fidget

Now Fidget was basking in his accomplishment when he was motioned by Fussy. Waving her hands slowly and pointing to the inside of the kitchen, she mouthed an Okay with wide eyes. Fidget slowly scanned the room when a movement caught his eye. In the dark room, on the darker floor, moved the darkest of forms. Slowly it stood up and Fidget saw the outline of old Rattler, the house's dog. His high pitched whistle to Swoop had been heard by the dog and had awakened him.

Rattler stretched out his front legs as he put his big yawning head in its sleep pose like all dogs do. He began to turn around in the place by the stove several times and lay back down. One more gigantic yawn with his head and then he closed his eyes to go asleep. The Smidgens began to breath again, slowly. They now had to contend with a plastic screen over the window, old Rattler and the unknown location of Jump.

The Smidgens watched the grumpy owners of the blue-green house get tired of bickering and walk out of the living room. "They must be going to bed," said Fussy.

"Yes." Replied Fidget and we should nap some too, for a short time."

Lights out and quiet pervaded the entire structure. The moon peaked out again from its cloudy curtains, bathing the landscape with golden light. The two little people waited for the light in the sky to hide, and then they came together for a conference.

"He is not in any of the three rooms," opined Fidget.

"And yet we saw him enter and not leave. He must be in a closet or cupboard. Let's try to get in and investigate that closet and see whether we can locate Jump," Fussy commented.

"Let's just do it," said Fidget as the moon once again greeted their endeavors. The trees swayed in a gentle breeze as if in agreement and even the grasses in the yard below shifted or moved in apparent excitement.

CHAPTER
NINETEEN

Mater gently guided Empire to the library and had him sit down in his favorite chair. "We have much to discuss. I want to proceed now and permit Golly Gee to our meeting to clarify any items that need interpretation. I believe Mr. Snooty, and his spurious buyers for the mansion are not what they seem to be. I'll be back in a moment and while I am gone, you can go over the papers that were originally presented us. Then reflect on their conduct in the final minutes of their most recent stay." With Empire 's mouth trying to speak, "what's going on? " These papers are the contracts for Rustic Realm's sale"

"Yes" said, Mater. Read them and see if you can find out if we are being cheated or scammed. Mater quickly pivoted on her foot and headed for a meeting with Golly Gee.

Down the great hall, she exited towards the Parlor. Mater moved with an aroma of power and a sure mission in her wake. She was soon in the presence of Golly and Bakka in the parlor. Golly Gee had been tidying-up, and Bakka was helping. Dusting and arranging some of the furniture, they stopped and waited for Mater to speak.

She looked directly at Golly and said, "I'll need you to help me talk to and convince my husband of the things we know and suspect. Bakka can come also if you think she will be able to add to the information that we have discussed." Mater's sparkling gray eyes scanned both women as they shortly paused during the thinking process.

Golly spoke with authority in her own right. "I think it best if I go with you, and Bakka can stay here and keep eyes and ears open with Redd Peppers, for our little adventurous friends who are still not back from their trip. The more I think about the whole situation, the more concerned I am about their journey and the evil they may run into. My hope is that they will return soon. Let's go and tell Mr. Uppity all that we know and encourage him to try to get the authorities involved again."

With those words, the two women left the Parlor. Bakka went to the pantry and kitchen and would use the intercom to bring Redd up to date on all the happenings.

Mater spoke with an openness that surprised Golly "I also have a feeling of impending misfortune if we don't act quickly. Only now do I correctly comprehend the evil these three people brought to our house. It is as though I have been awakened from a long sleep. My depression over the loss of Jump made everything fuzzy and out of reach. I can see now more than my eyes report to me."

"We must convince my husband of the urgency to act even if it is only because of our feelings and suspicions," Mater ended her dialogue as she reached the library door first.

They inconspicuously approached Mr. Uppity who was sitting in his great leather chair in the library. On his lap lay some papers. He was holding his head up by his right hand. A finger on his mustaches and a thumb under hid chin his, was the grand study of deep thoughtfulness and reflection. His breathing was alternating with deep sighs of concern and revelation. His wrinkled brow and his softly pushed back gray hair were signs of doubt. He was a man on the cutting edge of a decision, needing only the slightest provocation for action.

"I can see now that they made fools of me", Empire spoke with thin conviction, but sufficient to make an accurate decision." Mr. Uppity didn't move. He spoke with no one particularly. He knew his wife and housekeeper where in the room.

A large gilded mirror over one of the sofas had given him their reflection in a micro glance seconds earlier. "Their persistence and directness, coupled with my grief, took me off guard. They were too eager to acquiesce to my demands. Too ready to be agreeable to all conditions. Money appeared to be no obstacle."

"Sweet words, smooth gestures to a grieving Father pulled the wool over my eyes", emotionally spent he paused.

Mater instinctively began to massage his back and shoulders. His arm dropped, and his head sagged forward at her relaxing and gentle movements. Before he could continue Mater spoke lovingly.

"Dear, we need to tell you everything we know and suspect. I've brought Golly to tell you first hand all that has happened in the recent past. Some of these things will be hard to believe, but Jump's life may hang in the balance."

What followed was two women telling all. Golly Gee went first. Standing before the master of the house, as a sergeant reporting to the General, she told all about the Smidgens and their most recent flights.

"What! Have there been foreign beings running around our house without us knowing about them?"

His eyebrows moved to a perplex position of shock. "I can't believe all this has been happening under my nose. Are you sure of these conclusions?"

With only a deep breath and a nod of her head she continued.

She told of all the things she had seen and heard when the Pinchings and Mr. Snooty came to the house. She told of the impressions that Redd Peppers formed (that he had shared with her), when he was chauffeuring the group back and forth from town.

Empire was drinking in all this in with wide eyes and slacked jaw. It was too difficult to believe all at once, he thought. "I sure would like to see one. Are they bigger than a bug?"

"You will see them soon Empire," Mater said as she went on to relate all of her feelings and impressions once she had heard about the little dark blue-green house in the deep woods. Hope had leapt out and grabbed her when told about the little Smidgens first flight. "It began to give me intuition about these strangers that wanted our house and grounds for possible illicit reasons," she continued.

"We really didn't actively want to sell, but we had casually mentioned it at some social gatherings and then Mr. Snooty began his intense campaign to have us sell. It was all like a movie that was being shown before us but not happening to us." Mater concluded by saying, "I think Jump is in the hands of these people and possibly in the blue-green house as a prisoner. I know it is only an impression but it is so vivid I can't let it go. We must be very careful because now if we make one false move they could exterminate him because he is a witness to their villainous activities."

Both of the ladies discourses were interrupted occasionally by Mr. Uppity's rapid-fire bursts of, "but, but!" They stayed the course and eventually looked at him with eyes of anticipation.

After a short pause Empire said, "If all these things are true and your hunches are correct we should go to the police and inform them. However, most of it is unbelievable and unsubstantiated. They might ridicule us and want more time for investigating and collecting information. In the interim the crooks may hear of the inquiries and do something foolish and irreparable. We can't on our own just find whether the little blue-green house exists and go barging in. That would also be too dangerous. What do you think Ms. Gee?"

Golly Gee was standing while intently listening and sank into the empty massive brown sofa again without asking permission. The air was filled with the mutual bonding of allies.

"Mr. Uppity I will see that one or more of the Smidgens will make themselves known to you a little later on." Golly continued. "I thought that we would wait for the hopeful return of the little Smidgens, the Bright Ones, to determine if what we believe is true. We could also add to our information, things such as: lay out and numbers etc."

"Also, I would strongly suggest that no mention of the little Smidgens be made to any other persons. Outsiders as well as the official authorities wouldn't be helped by this revelation. The Little People need their autonomy for their very survival. A strategic and calculated phone call to the authorities would be applicable as we wait until the anticipated return of the two Smidgens later."

"I don't think I can wait that long before doing something," said Mater. Maybe you could introduce me to the other Smidgens so that I could fortify my convictions in this entire incident. I am sure that Mr. Uppity has some phone calls to make, unless you want to come with us, dear?"

Mater looked over at her husband for a response. He still looked dazed but did exhibit a new resolve about his mouth that had been missing for months. He looked at them both and smiled.

"You're not just making all this up", he said in a playful manner as he rose from his chair and stretched. "You two go ahead and I'll try to join you later. I think now that I will call our attorney and a close friend of mine in the Police Department who is a detective. My hope is that they won't want too many details of a delicate nature.

We will wait until nightfall before initiating any

action on the blue-green house or on the scoundrels involved in this suspicious, quickie real estate deal."

The little group smiled at each other and walked out of the library to fulfill the tasks described and to wait. A waiting game with possible life or death consequences.

CHAPTER
TWENTY

*T*he moon played peek-a-boo with the drifting clouds, affording occasional quality light, mingled with near darkness. It would make the night's work spastic and dangerous. Fidget began to carefully cut the screen that was tacked to the window sash. It was pliable and easier to cut than first thought. The going was slow because of the SNAP at the end of each cut.

Fidget was acutely aware of the viciousness of the occupants within. No need to wake a pack of naughties. If one is slow and deliberate, one can accomplish much without any ado. This was easier than trying to pry away the screen that was tightly tacked. That was the first option tried. Fussy was able to hold up the snipped portion of screen after a short while, thereby enlarging the opening until it appeared that the small bodies of the Smidgens could conveniently pass through. With nods and gestures, accompanied by lithe movements, the two wee ones moved through the screen and settled themselves on the inside window ledge. It was a time to observe and listen. All four eyes were now accustomed to the dim light of the late hour and deserted space before them. They scanned the room for signs and future opportunities. The kitchen was a hodgepodge of shapes. Sink, table, desk, stove, refrigerator, shelves, sleeping dog, the archway to the front room, and there was a closed door, next to floor to ceiling cupboards. Maybe a pantry, a broom closet, or other possibilities.

The two investigators looked at each other and then pointed to the closed broom closet door while nodding their heads in agreement. With air-like skill, the two proceeded to leap to the sink and then to a chair and finally to the floor. Their soft, leather footgear making no sound whatsoever, permitting them to move as their forefathers must have done in days of old.

Wide eyes looked continuously at the carnivorous canine, as the pair started towards the door, as the moon played peek-a-boo. The room was flooded with creamy moonlight and playfully spotlighted the two in mid-step. They froze. The object of their concern shook and reached for some imaginary foe as lips drew back and teeth bared complete with a low throaty growl.

They both relaxed as deep sleep returned to the shaggy headed dog as the moon played, Peek-a-Boo with light drifting into to kitchen area making the room more visible to any searching eyes. The light slowly retreated, and the cloak of darkness again covered the covert operation. Quiet leather clad feet again proceeded towards the closet door.

Reaching the target, the Smidgens crouched down so that the doorsill gap was used to listen for any signs of life. With generous ears, the two prepared to catch any movement or sound. Each little life held their breath to more accurately to hear any telltale sounds.

"Yes, it is the sound of faint breathing on the other side of the door. Let's hope it is not another animal," whispered Fussy as she proceeded to point to the key in the lock of the door.

"I'll lasso it and pull it out and you catch it," replied Fidget quietly, as he unwound his rope and prepared to cast it up to his target.

With agreement, they laid their packs on either side of Fussy, the catcher, in case of a fumble. She positioned herself underneath the key and signaled Fidget she was ready.

Fidget would have to throw the rope while close to the door and when coiled securely about the key shaft, he would then would walk away from the door to near the center of the room, thereby pulling the key out of the keyhole. With hand signals indications and head nods, each knew the procedure and thumbs up paved the way for beginnings.

The miniature rope was twirled and thrown up to the protruding key. The first cast was too short. Fidget retrieved the front end of the rope and put more knots in it for added weight to better reach the needed key. Fussy checked on old Rattler still sleeping and waved approval for another try.

Fidget sent the lasso up and over the key in a fluid motion that made the knotted end revolve several times about the key's shaft. The line was secured with a gentle tug. Fidget, keeping the line taut and slowly working his way toward the center of the room, was a difficulty. He was constantly aware of the dog, making the advance very slow but deliberate.

Fidget wondered if a quick pull and get it over with or a slow pull, allowing for adjustments would be best. No time for too much consideration. A slow tug to see whether it was loose. It was. Now a quick pull to get it over with. Out it came from its keyhole, tumbling down to the waiting arms of the catcher. Completed pass. First down. Big smiles.

The next part of the plan was to try to awaken the locked occupant and determine its identity. If it was Jump, the key would be passed under the door for the start of the great escape, if not, they would just turn around and leave telling all to Golly Gee back home.

Fidget remained the lookout as Fussy lay down at the gap between floor and door and began to whisper. "Jump, is that you in there? Hello Jump. It's I, Fussy, one of the Smidgens from Rustic Manor."

No answer. The closet was quiet as a tomb. *Where was Jump?*

Eventually a sound of a body turning and of interrupted breathing from within gave a good clue. Fussy repeated her message and added a few more decibels. There was a stirring from inside the closet. A clearing of the throat and then quiet. Fussy tried the third time with a deeper voice and her face and mouth pressed further into the gap under the door. Her enunciation with clear tones finally reached sleepy ears.

"What? Say that again. Who is there?" came a young sleepy voice from a surprised Jump.

"It's Fidget and Fussy. We've come to rescue you. Be very quiet. We are going to pass the key to the door through this crack so you can carefully open the door. Do you understand?"

The voice came back and was so filled with emotion it almost cracked. "I've waited so long. I can hardly believe it's you. I been so unhappy and tired and...."

Fussy knowing that tears would soon follow interrupted and again gave the orders and directions for the plan. "Be quiet and slow. Open the door slowly so old Rattler doesn't awake," Fussy admonished. She waited for an "Okay", and then got up and whispered to fidget all that was said. They put their packs back on and waited next to the door jam.

Peek, went the moon as it again invaded the kitchen with silvery light, giving its self to the advantage of owners instead of intruders. It was not so bright this time because clouds moved through the sky to reveal other sights to other searching eyes.

The key was inserted into the lock on the other side of the door and it made metallic scrapping noises as the lock gave way.

A crisp click of the mechanism declared its condition. Unlocked! The sound traveled through the house without an echo and apparently did not disturb any slumbering inhabitants. Even so, a Smidgen was at the closet door opening, giving the newly freed prisoner the whispered "hush" and the sign of finger to lips.

It was Jump as expected. Now older and thinner. The months here had cost him a slice of youth and innocence. One could tell by the drawn lines of the face and the heavy eyes, looking for deliverance for days on end. Thin lips, unkempt hair, and stooped shoulders completed the picture. A gaunt boy but still it was the Jump of Rustic realm. Jump was still wearing his clothes as he usually did. He was required to be "up and at'em," every morning in a matter of a minute or two or suffer the blows of the irritable Nastine. He pushed into his shoes easily because they were worn out with tattered shoestrings and well-worn leather. He bent his head down to be closer to his two benefactors and to get a better look.

A whispered, "thanks," was heard as a smile crossed the young boy's face for the first time in almost a year. The face remembered the smile sequence but it came off with some difficulty. Before any more dialogue could be exchanged the little people pointed to the door and indicted exiting. All was understood as the three slowly and silently glided toward the back door. Jump put his hand on the door knob and turned. It was locked. No key in the door. Jump remembered it was always locked.

All of his keyhole observations were not in vain. The two Smidgens wondered and were puzzled as Jump reached for a cookie jar. *How could he be hungry at a time like this when all our efforts could be thwarted by a locked door,* 'thought Fussy? Rustling noises. Metal clinking against cookie jar. A key produced and held up as a prize by one jubilant Jump. He placed it in the lock and turned. The lock gave way and the door released. Jump had the door open and moved pass the screen door and took a deep breath of free air. Gently closing that noisy screen door jump tried hard to contain his feelings of his newfound freedom The two tiny colleagues motioned towards a great yard tree where they would meet before taking of in the woods.

Behind the tree the reunion was completed with minuscule hugs and words of endearment. "Rustic Manor is far away. We can reach it by going down a fence row, through the big woods to the trout stream, right at the stream and them up the fields to the great lawn and then we are home," said Fidget. He continued, "we must leave now and travel all night because our progress will be slowed by the darkness. I'll get our moths, and we can go together. We'll lead the way, and you can follow. If we get separated we will use low whistling to relocate each other. The moonlight is still good enough to get us far away from here," Fidget concluded.

Fussy was still wiping away tears of joy as Fidget raised his fingers for the whistled signal that would bring the moths to them. He blew hard even though it appeared as though no sound were emitted. A slight movement could be seen on the roof as the two moths stretched their wings and prepared for the descent to the designated area. They lifted off and commenced the short flight down to the waiting Smidgens.

Grating sounds came from the kitchen that they had just left. Through the back door and screen door, they could hear the sounds turning to a low growl.

"Oh my," said Fussy, "your high pitched whistle also disturbed old Rattler. The growling paralleled those of a big old hunting dog, awaking fresh with blood on his mind and odor in his nose. "Run Jump! Straight ahead to the fencerow and then home. We will try to delay any attempt the dog may have of following you. Go!"

The newly freed lad moved like a frightened rabbit and was quickly near the woods. Running on adrenalin the small boy appeared to be gliding over the grassy area and soon purchased an oneness with the forest. Jump's shoes were on tight because of his growth spurt while a prisoner.

The noise in the house increased from growls to deep base barking that resembled a hound hot on the scent. The sounds were almost declaring pain and grief. The two moths had landed and were inspected, loaded and then instantly mounted. It all only took a matter of seconds as the Smidgens began to follow Jump into the great woods.

Yet in that time the lights were on in the bedroom and then glowed in the kitchen. Old rattler had advanced with his nose pressed to the screen door and was moaning with explosive viciousness.

Shouting oaths filled the night air, mingled with the incessant howling of the old hunting dog gave the scene a nightmarish quality. Curses, the sounds of slamming doors and breaking glass added to the seething brew in the house. Finally, quiet tried to prevail, except for the baleful canine calling. Voices cut the air.

"He's gone! He's gone!

"How?" Each gravely gruff voice taking a turn. "I don't know how, you twit! He's just gone."

The words sounded nasty. The bear-like man barked, "don't just stand there, open the door, and let old Rattler have a go at him." The command snarled as loud as the dog's yapping.

The night was well spent. The moon had moved further off to the horizon and was giving forth less light than several hours ago. The wind had picked up slightly. It made the top of the trees rustle.

As the wind began to increase, the limbs and boughs

moved and swayed in synchronization with the great heavenly baton. Even the grasses moved suspiciously. The temperature had dropped slightly and could be described as brisk but not cold. A few rumblings could be heard far off where heat lightening tested its showy manner.

The man and dog intended an intrusion of the woods and began to spew forth its venom on this peaceful sight. The screen door flew open, and the great hunter ceased his yelping as he put his cold black nose to the ground. "Go get'em," came the voice of Bark Gruffly on the heels of his nighttime prowler.

The experienced old warrior-hound bounded through the yard, hot on the scent of the once orphaned, once adopted, once kidnapped, now freed little boy.

This entire scene had not gone unnoticed by the two bright minds of the inventive Smidgens. Only minutes before they had anticipated the eruption of force and the resulting pursuit. With speed and inborn agility they had taken their rope and tied it across the probable path of the pursuers.

With the one end tied to a tree trunk and the other knotted end in their hands they allowed the rope to lie on the ground until the appropriate moment.

"Keep behind the tree and just before old Rattler comes bounding along we will pull with all our might to trip him," Fidget said anxiously.

"Then what?" Was the query of Fussy with a quiver in her voice?

"When he gets up we will have enough time to mount the moths and take off," was the answer of Fidget in his confident manner.

Fussy then looked anxiously at the two waiting moths.

"Sure, that old dog will be so discombobulated that it will take him a minute to reorient himself. By then we will be off and join up with Jump. Here comes the old bag of bones now." Fidget concluded by griping the rope more tightly; ready to pull it tight over the pathway.

The light from the kitchen behind the rushing Rattler made him look more menacing and meaner than was the sleeping guard on the kitchen floor. A black cloud, of ghostly quality, bellowed as though his tail were caught under the rail of a rocking chair. Straight for the Smidgens, on the trail of a freed boy's feet came Old Rattler with prominent nose, mouth, and teeth. His eyes in the fading moonlight were like burning pinpoints of red-hot heat but yellow in hated. He didn't see what his feet felt. The Bright Ones had executed their plan.

Over he went, feet in the air, cessation of howling, the tracker disengaged, as though a toy thrown in the air. He hit a lilac bush and went deep within its foliage. In a split second the limber bush had moved him back out and catapulted directly towards the two instigators. Before they could reach, their respective moth rides into the realm of safety, the bag of muscles and bones landed directly in front of them on all fours. His eyes now flashed amber as he immediately regained his senses and confronted his prey. His gaping mouth opened wider, and gleaming canine teeth protruded. His body tensed for the lunge forward to annihilate his prize.

Size meant nothing to him. Large or small. He had seen them all. Mice, rabbits, birds, and even deer. All the defenseless forest creatures in the big woods were easy pickings

The Smidgens were shortly stunned by this turn of events. Just as they where turning to flea, a screeching noise of ear shattering proportions was heard from the menacing canine. The cry of a banshee couldn't have sent more shivers up the spine of the listeners. Out of the grass and through the night vapors came a pair of slit yellow eyes that guided four paws with claws extended and feline fangs of frightening potential. The aerial maneuver of the impending feline intruder checked the hound's advance.

The shrill battle cry of Rattler intensified as the author of feline domination landed on the back and neck of the puzzled and now frozen-like dog.

Peyton began his attack on sensitive ears and then the nose. The great beast below Peyton was befuddled and went to the ground in defense. Peyton still on top as Rattler pawed the air with eyes shut. The black cat with the white tipped tail flailing the air looked at the Smidgens and then the place where Jump had disappeared into the woods, all in a split second.

The two tiny people knew at once that the glance spoke volumes. While Peyton continued to incapacitate the hound, Fidget and Fussy mounted Swoop and Glide. Off they went towards the fencerow and down the hill to the trout stream where Jump would probably be waiting.

The moths went quite fast at first but now slowed, since entering the great woods. Their eyes were accustomed to the dark surroundings of the forest, especially since the moon was on the wane. Their Goggles were off. The moths were comfortable in their own environment. They moved with their precious cargo with their expert characteristics.

Darkness enveloped the four escaping figures as sounds in the background indicated a retreating bully and a victorious house pet.

CHAPTER

TWENTY ONE

ustic Realm hummed with activity through the wee hours. Like busy bees the occupants each went in different but symbiotic directions. Golly introduced Mater to the Smidgen community after much cajoling and encouragement involving the little people.

A short time later Golly left this small but growing love feast and headed towards the kitchen and Bakka Bean's domain. Bakka told Golly that her searching the grounds for the two bright Smidgens and their moths came to naught. "The Bright Ones should be back by now. We all are praying for their safe return and fruitful report." She confided that Redd Peppers was also helping by positioning himself down by the woods to see whether he could possibly see or hear them coming back to Rustic Realm while waiting perfectly still. He came back once for some coffee and had reported no success. "I am going to stay down there even if it means an all-night vigil," said Redd as he excited the kitchen.

"He returned to that post only minutes ago and said he would be back in several hours," reported Bakka to Golly Gee.

Golly finally sat down in one of the kitchen chairs as Bakka poured her a large cup of freshly brewed coffee. Bakka did the same for herself and the klatch was completed. Two heads moved closer over the table as Golly began to tell of the meeting she had with the Uppitys. "Mr. Uppity was sure surprised about the Smidgens but didn't appear upset about the whole picture of little people and their friends in and around the house. Empire was getting the Authorities involved with a hope that Jump could be found over in the deep woods. He was calling several people that could help in this situation as I left."

Bakka's dark eyes grew large as the events unfolded verbally before her and she realized as the others had, that hope was slowly being transformed into faith and eventually some action.

Their eyes sparkled in unison as Golly told of the meeting of Smidgens and Mater. "Mater had a real get-together with some of the Smidgens that was most beautiful and touching for her and the little people." Warm, full smiles revealed again the delight when they where first introduced to these diminutive people. More smiles and soft laughter permeated the room as the two ladies reminisced about past encounters and events with the Smidgens. Hands touching in recognition, heads nodding in agreement, chair shifting in accentuation, the pair lived these special times to the fullest, not knowing when the opportunity might again avail itself. The time flew by and it was late.

Bakka was to keep on the look-out for the two fliers and report if Redd had any news. Golly indicated that late-night visitors might be possible. Coffee and sandwiches would be appreciated.

"Can do," came the spirited reply. "I must also keep an eye out for Peyton.

He hasn't touched any of the food that I've placed for him, and I have not seen him all day. I don't know whether to be worried or not. It is unusual for him to out all night. I think he was last seen skulking around the garden outside looking for mischief of some sort. I am sure that even in his rambunctious ways with the Smidgens he would never actually hurt them. Ever since Jump came to live here the cat changed somewhat. He is mostly macho cat with puff and pounces but with domesticated breeding. More of a tease than a felonious feline. Jump always loved him and played for hours in the yard with him."

"Oh, he will return. He is a smart cat. A little jealous when Jump would spend time with the wee folk. I don't think there is a connection since Peyton has stayed out all night before. Be sure to tell Redd about it and keep his eyes and ears open for the cat also."

Golly got up from the table slowly and with a pleasant face said she would leave and see to the needs of the Uppitys. If any new developments arose she would report as soon as possible. Each looked at their empty coffee cups and then to the kitchen clock and finally at each other as they acknowledged by eye contact, the preciousness of the time spent. With straightening and smoothing motions of hair and dress, each returned to the air of their positions and departed from the meeting.

Golly moved quickly with squared shoulders, through the pantry and down a little passage way to the backstairs. Only the narrowness and winding of the stairs kept Golly from taking the steps two at a time.

With the new found physical energy pouring into her body she literally flew down the upstairs hallway to the room she had left Mater Uppity and the Smidgens.

Even before entering the room she could feel the vigor and exuberance of the gathering. She silently entered the room and beheld on the floor the lady of the house in intense, animated discussions with a myriad of bright eyed little people. Their smallness and her rank had not deterred the creation of good fellowship and camaraderie. It was almost a shame to interrupt. Mater on her knees and haunches with Smidgens chattering all about her. She returned the dialogue as fast as she could form the words and phrases. Some of the folks were on her shoulders, in her pockets, one was held in her hand and the rest acted like Mexican jumping beans in front of her to draw her attention and to extract her replies.

Graybub was in front with Oldene by his side, giving her ear all the exercise that his machine-gun fire oracles could generate. They were trying to convince her of this and that and seemed to be making some headway.

Mater was enjoying every bit of it in her motherly way. The deep lines that had been on her face had smoothed out with the soft glow of contentment and expectation. Clear eyes and vibrant expressions with gentle hand movements completed the picture of the revitalized Mrs. Mater Uppity.

Golly gently interrupted this scene to tell Mater that the night was late and that it would be prudent if they returned to the first floor and determined what progress Mr. Uppity had made and if they could be of any assistance to him. Mater nodded in agreement and slowly released from her hand the irascible Flippant who had talked non stop since being recognized and held up. Startled, he removed himself from her grasp and began to tell all, that he had persuaded and convinced Mrs. Uppity to think upon his numerous suggestions.

Golly helped Mater to her feet and silently left the room as the discussions were now centered on Flippant, Graybub, and Oldene. Small talk would be enlarged.

The two ladies proceeded at the late hour down the front stairs and located Empire in the study or the SNUG as Mater occasionally called it. The room was substantial but filled with warm dark woods and comfortable furniture, thereby living up to both its names.

It sounded as though Empire were just finalizing one of his phone calls. He had made notes on a large yellow legal pad and one could see that several previous calls had demanded many lines and some doodling. He completed the call and disconnected. With a great sigh of relief he tapped the legal pad with the pencil and then sat down in his big comfortable, overstuffed leather chair.

His left hand stroked under his chin, checking for stubble and soothing the vocal cords with one pass. He looked up and spoke with his intent audience.

"I've been on the phone ever since you left, and have made calls and received calls. I believe the lid is about to come off and answers will soon start to flow. I had a nice long talk with our attorney first, to get his advice and counsel. I then called my detective friend on the local police force. He listened to our suspicions and since the case was still open he assured me he would immediately begin to investigate. He thought some of the names could be run through the computers and a few phone calls on his part may jog someone's memory. I called Judge Tough and asked whether he would give the police access to deeds and records at the courthouse if they needed to do some research.

He said it was irregular but since it appeared to involve the kidnapping he would be available for any legal warrants or searches and such like. Just now the detective called and informed me of their progress which was considerable. They had even made calls to the STRANGEVILLE police. Profiles and aliases began to pop up everywhere on their computers, he said. Connections have been made. A large amount of money has been located, and methods discovered.

"It appears a web of crime may be the cause of Jump's disappearance," he ended by saying, "that as soon as all the legal details and plan particulars are jelled, the officials would come here and discuss their next move. Since that might mean a raid on the little blue-green house they would like to confer with us about the possible discovery of Jump at that location and the inherent dangers." With a final sigh of exhaustion he relaxed and allowed the chair to envelope him and concluded, "what do you think?"

Both females of the moment, seeing an opportunity to release both wisdom and emotion moved forward on their respective chairs while drawing in deep breaths for endurance. They looked at each other and recognized the starters gun and the need for the younger to yield to the elder. It was done in an instant.

Golly exhaling and slightly retreating into her chair, while Mater began to utter a flutter of words of relief and positive ness.

"This is it. I can feel it. My Jump will be home tomorrow. Tell your detective to come and bring all the troops he can muster. He can arrest those miscreants and take the whole lot of them to jail. We will have coffee and sandwiches and make a plan to find this blue-green house and bring our boy home."

Chapter

TWENTY TWO

The night was well spent and so was the moon and it's pleasant luminescence. The moths moved through the woods with the two Smidgens holding on tightly in case of any low branches and grabby green briar underbrush. The eyes of the great moths quickly acclimated to the reduced light. By nature they would seek out any light source ahead and fly in that direction. Little or no light was available, except the melting moon and an occasional fire fly. This made the moths want to fly towards the light source when seen.

Therefore the Smidgens had to fight to stay the course. Their duty was to stay low, trying to intercept their fleeing friend so recently freed. The rushing of wind in their commodious ears smothered all noise behind them. No time to stop and listen for possible pursuers yet.

The moths agilely moved through and about the

bushes and boles of the forest's trees and vegetative covering. They continued this forward progress much like the bowling ball heading toward the seven-ten split on league night.

Fussy began to think of the next step in the rescue. For some reason this part of the event was never really discussed in detail. It always seemed when some sort of success was reached that the plans began to dissipate because of the great relief and the flooding in of emotions. One must be careful not to leave this course of action until the entire plan is fulfilled. 'Plan your work, work your plan,' was a saying of the Smidgens. Fussy knew that they would have to reign up soon and evaluate their position and determine their plans of action. That would take time and would not be as relieving as flying towards home, but good plans based on fact and faith were the essence of success.

Graybub once told her that, she thought, as she tried to make contact with Fidget to find a place to land so that they could listen and evaluate their surroundings.

Fussy encouraged Glide to quicken his pace and finally through the low whistles of the Smidgen clan was able to get the attention of Fidget. His head had been low and had been surely bent on getting along as fast as possible.

His face expressed doubt in the wisdom of a landing but soon reflected on the erudition of his partner, both past and present. Fidget signaled in the affirmative and allowed Fussy to pass to select the landing sight.

They were both gliding towards a large branch of a tree that was low enough for observing and high enough for safety. They landed. In hushed tones Fidget suggested that one try to listen towards the fence line for Jump's movements, and the other one listen for any pursuers. In agreement they each dismounted and moved slightly in the direction of their individual target to enhance their objective and then stood still. The night had worn thin and been rather still. The smallest of breezes would gently rise and fall. A few leaves did flutter and move as though stretching for coming of the dawn.

Each listener cupped a hand to their ample ears to catch the tiniest of sounds that would give them hints of how to proceed.

A sound pierced the night, like a cold knife thrust into the heart. It wasn't very near but told a story of a baying hound again on the trail. The two Smidgens returned to each other and in a quick meeting determined that Jump's movements were not detected, but old Rattler's movements were.

"We must continue on and assume that Jump has been able to follow our recommended directions and is still way ahead." Fidget continued. "I have seen some fire flies and suggest we capture a few in flight in case we catch up to Jump. We can use them for beacons for him to follow in some of the more dangerous zones in total darkness."

"We must be very careful," added Fussy. "I saw some lingering bats on the prowl as we came through that last section of woods. They should be leaving the woods and heading towards the fields for insects, then to their home as dawn begins to unfold."

"We must be on the alert for them and try to find a place in the trout stream for all of us to cross that will stymie that malicious hound."

"Our plan is to hurry and catch Jump before he reaches the stream. You catch some fireflies and we must confound that dog too. I think if I fly to that small bush over there and vault to the ground and run around it and several others close by touching them to leave my scent in a circular pattern, then climb a bush and fly off. That might confuse old snaggletooth." Fidget puffed out his tiny chest as he finished and waited for his friend's approval.

With a nod of her head, Fussy concurred. "You do the bit about the bush and I'll go ahead slowly and catch some fireflies and put them in my little clear bottle and then we will meet down at the end of the fence row as it meets the trout stream.

Do be careful! I think I can hear that yelping getting closer so he must be on track."

With a little hug and peck on the cheek, the two remounted and went their separate ways to implement their plan.

Fidget landed smoothly on the designated bush and then gave instructions to Swoop to stay put as he leaped to the ground and began his circling of bushes and trees. He reached out and touched every thing in sight as he quickly moved to complete his assigned task. Pulling leaves, rubbing tree trunks as he ringed them, the task was varied by even rolling around on the ground. After this he returned to the first bush and moved up through the twigs to the waiting moth.

Then, they were both airborne and on their way through the rest of the woods and to the fence row. Up ahead Fidget could see that Fussy had secured several of the blinking, lightning bugs. She was moving in a straight line down the hill towards the stream. As he caught up, he could hear in the background the newer, high-pitched baying of a hound that had treed an invisible victim. Success, thought Fidget as he waved them on to the stream in the cool, sparse starlight.

Jump was just getting out of the stream that he had tried to ford but without success. He had been hidden him from their view until the last second.

He was wet and tired but he slowly walked the stream to find another way across. The two Smidgens spotted him at the same time and flew in close. "Jump. Jump!" They called to him to get his attention so they could land on his shoulder.

They needed a concluding confabulation before his final dash to freedom. He looked up in surprise but also relief. His little face was both wet with water and with tears. His stark face spoke of the terror he had endured over the last year. Revelation knowledge of what could happen if he did not succeed in his race to get home was written in capital letters on the underfed features of Jump. A mere seconds hesitation swept aside, and a motion to proceed was what the two Bright Ones were looking for.

Glide landed with Fussy on the left shoulder of the shivering boy. Fidget steered Swoop to his right shoulder for a pleasant landing.

"Jump, we are halfway home. All we have to do is find a good place to cross the stream that would confuse old Rattler and then its smooth sailing back to Rustic Realm. I have captured some fireflies so that you can follow us and not get lost in this endeavor, the most difficult part of this trek." Fussy then showed the three fireflies, healthy, blinking and winking and nodding.

"I am so cold and tired I don't know how much more I can go. My shoes keep slipping around with the water and I feel so tired that sometimes I am dizzy. My stomach hurts, and I am scratches head to toe. I am so glad you guys came and got me out of there. One more week and I think I would have been done in or even done away with by them. I am so happy and yet so tired. Am I making any sense?"

Fidget cleared his throat and his finest counseling voice said, "you can make it. Your Mom and Dad are just less than a mile away and not a thousand. You have two friends to help you through the night. You are young and strong within because of how you can think. Think of the good things to come. Think about how much endurance you have shown already tonight. All things are possible to those that believe. Let's go forward. You follow the fireflies that Fussy has, and I will be behind you as a sentinel. We can go slow and steady and cover lots of ground before daylight."

It was not easy for Fidget to spill out all these words of advice and encouragement. He had known defeat and failure in his young life. Nevertheless, if he had learned anything in the counsel of his elders, it was that winners never quit. Try, try, and try again was his personal motto.

With wide-eyed nods of agreement, Fussy slowly had her moth take off down the stream with Jump coming behind her. Fidget brought up the rear. The little party moved down along the stream bank and came to a part that was wide. It was not too deep at first so that Jump could just wade in. About three fourths away across, the stream had made a deep channel. Here was a place one could jump up on a big rock and then vault to shore in a giant leap.

Jump followed Fussy and lived up to his name as he landed on the far side of the stream, where he fell down to rest. He had accomplished a great feat. They used two diversion tactics that would keep the canine pursuer from interfering with an inevitable reunion.

Off in the distance, upon a wooded hill, the incessant cry of an intense hound at work in circles could be heard.

A few minutes of well-earned rest could be expended now that home was closer by a stream width. This deep in the woods the surroundings were very dark and at every turn an imagined enemy could be almost detected by alert Smidgen eyes. Jump had his closed in the ecstasy of release and relief.

"Not home yet." said Fussy as she noticed the anemic light production of her captive firefly charges. "Time to release these and get three more," she said to Fidget who was close to the ground, listening to far off sounds.

"Sure thing," replied Fidget. "You get three more fireflies and I'll stay here and keep watch as Jump catches his breath and renews his strength. Be as quick as you can so that we don't take for granted some of our successes already in place. Our ability to avoid trouble on this return trip has been very good. Let's not try to stretch any activities to the point we lose that advantage."

Off she went with her moth, releasing the three fireflies on the wing. They were all in good condition, other than some of their might had gone out of their light.

Fidget spied a bat, but it was leaving the forest and was alone. It was heading for home surmised Fidget. When the bats were gone and the birds had not yet taken to flight, their plan was to fly back up to Rustic Realm. The minutes were very important.

Fidget saw Fussy returning in the dark, blinking again brightly. Like a wishing star fulfilling its destiny, she returned to his side as effortlessly as a good morning kiss. The two began to arouse Jump to full wakefulness and then to stand up and continue the trek through the woods.

"I'm up. I'm up. What happened? I feel better," he said as he stood to regain his position in the middle of the little procession.

Fussy complete with full winking force, led them along past the great fields of planted crops. They all swiftly entered the manicured lawns of Rustic Realm.

"It won't be long now," uttered Fussy, over her shoulder. "Hurry up you guys."

Her enthusiasm was suddenly surrounded by something strong, and all encompassing force resulting in her forward motion being halted. A powerful force enveloped Fussy so strong but gentle. She couldn't move. The force seemed to close in on all sides of her being. 'So close,' she thought as the three new luminescence friends slipped away from her vial. Her hopes once so high were now plummeted to such depths that she began to faint. Total darkness was her reward for being first and very vocal. A dog? A cat, who knows?

Chapter

TWENTY THREE

The sharp knock on the great door was no surprise. The eyes of the house had noticed the arrival of the two vehicles some minutes before. Electric surveillance as well as anxious participants caught the plain looking four wheeled rigs making their way up to the front door and expelling a small group of plain looking men on a plain looking errand.

The great brass knocker was more apparent than the small door button to activate the bell. More striking too. With a prominent knock the door was of course opened instantly, and the greetings and invitations mingled quietly as entrance was made.

The tight little group moved effortlessly down the hall with introductions and formalities exchanged as smoothly as grandfather's pocket watch, ticking off the time. Golly closed the door and joined the group as she had instructed.

Six men wearing dark suits in need of pressing passed into the formal sitting room and were asked to be seated. Weary lines crisscrossed crossed their faces and accentuated their nearly day-old stubbles. Hats in hands, the men soon felt at ease with the urging of the hosts and one by one sat in strategically placed chairs. One man was left standing as the hosts sat on one of the large sofas. Golly sat in one of the straight back chairs near the door as her custom was. The man left standing was apparently in charge as he began to speak. Golly leaned forward to catch every word.

"Empire, all of your information has been most helpful. If these people are looked at one by one there appears to be no connection. When we put all of the names and occupations in place, it became apparent that some collusion was in our midst. Your realtor has a checkered past and his financial records are spurious at best. Some of his relatives have been charged with drug felonies and some of his properties have been found to house illegal handling of drugs. Your two prospective buyers are really from STRANGEVILLE, a place where the ransom call originated. They are known to have friends in the underworld. Two of their associates were busted over a year ago for manufacturing designer drugs and even some hard stuff. They skipped bond and haven't been seen since.

These two Grufflys in STRANGEVILLE were known to use local young toughs for their dirty work and would have to pay them off every so often to keep their mouths shut. We think it got too expensive for them to continue to do this and that is why we now believe they could have kidnapped your boy to use as grunt labor in their drug schemes. Cleaning utensils and providing menial labor free is the probable cause of your boy's kidnapping. That would cut down on the overhead for the two. A Mr. and Mrs. Gruffly with tempers and a lust for money are the ones we think may be holed up in that blue-green house you think may be on an unrecorded plot somewhere in your great woods. We have checked with Court records of deeds and plats and believe we know about where it is located. Years ago the state placed some fire roads in the big forests to facilitate any fire fighter efforts. The state has forgotten about most of the old roads. Never needed, never used."

The detective's mouth was getting dry and while he availed himself to the decanter of water set before him, the others whispered in agreement.

Empire asked, "what can we do now? Will six men be enough? When can we start?"

The detective resumed. "These men with me are all law officers plus an F.B.I agent. We have search warrants and at least two arrest warrants in the name of Gruffly. We are armed and are now waiting for a call. It's to let us know whether we can count on a helicopter for backup before we head in. This should take about ten more minutes to be sure all is place. We have a good idea where the fire road is. Before we came here, one of our group made several sorties into suspicious looking places along the old fire road. A suspicious opening in the woods is sure to be the old fire road. We are certain that it will lead us into the deep woods and to your blue-green house. I know of all of your concerns, but we feel that only Empire can come with us on this dangerous venture. He can be a calming effect on the boy if he is found. We are sorry Mrs. Uppity but feel that two parents would double the chances of someone getting hurt. We hope you understand."

"Of course, I understand. I will wait here while you make your foray into the dark and capture those evil persons and release my son."

Mater looked at Golly with a knowing eye. They both knew that the two little investigators where still not back from their flight. Nevertheless, neither lady had given way to fear or frustration.

"We have people ready to arrest the Pinchings, and also to take into custody Mr. Snooty upon our success with the Grufflys and their expected confessions. The prosecutor feels that we have enough to charge them and to send them all away for a long time."

The chief detective looked down at his shoes, trying to think of other things to say when Golly piped up.

"We have sandwiches and coffee out in the kitchen if anyone is interested."

It was the sunny announcement that broke the ice. All seemed to smile and concur as they rose from their places and began to nod their heads in agreement. They all slowly followed Golly like a gaggle of geese towards the kitchen for refreshments. Golly indicated where they were to be seated, around the dinette table to enjoy the handiwork of Bakka Bean's efforts.

Bakka floated about the company of law officers with an expertise that was efficiency itself. No cup left empty or any body wanting in her kitchen. The food was summarily depleted with satisfying remarks from all the men.

Suddenly the phone rang, and the chief answered with many "O.K." s and a few "yeps." He returned to the gathering and announced all was ready, and it was time to go. Like a navy blue- tide, the dark suits rose in unison and scurried to the front door where Empire stood excitedly waiting. The law and efficiency spilled into the waiting transportation and without any ado were off. The waves of goodbye by Mater, Golly, and Bakka continued until they had turned onto the main road and then disappeared.

The three returned to the inner part of the great house and ended up back in the kitchen. Mater sat down as though she had been wrung dry of her emotions for one day. Bakka busied herself with her duties with the cleanup and tidying of the area. Golly had gone to the back door and stood and looked out into the star-studded night.

"Where, oh where, are you little Smidgens," she spoke into the night air? "What have I allowed to happen to these gentle little folk?"

"Nothing that was not kind and good," came the reply from Mater as she positioned herself behind her friend and house manager.

"You were always trying to help look for Jump and keep the fires of hope alive."

These Smidgens, especially the two Bright Ones, needed to have freedom and the sanction of doing things while under your care. You gave it to them. No need to smother prepared and intelligent persons, no matter what their size. I'll need to remember that when Jump returns."

A comfortable smile came upon the face of Golly as she realized that the events of the past day had given her a real new friend in the person of Mater Uppity.

"It'll soon be daylight, and the dangers of the little flying duo will be increased," she said as she slowly turned to face her new friend. "How true," came the reply from Mater, birds and bumbles will again be on the prowl.

"Even so, we must not be over concerned if they don't show up. They are smart, quick, and willing to learn. Moreover, not always from experience only. I've spent many an hour teaching them about people and things that can be a threat. I told them that you don't have to be bitten by a shark to know they have sharp teeth." Golly had spent a lot of time with the Smidgen giving them counsel and wisdom. Her protégées picked up the wisdom like a dry sponge.

Mater listened with intense interest that was so consuming that the first shout was almost dismissed. Bakka heard it too and said, "what was that? " Listen."

Chapter

TWENTY FOUR

otal darkness for Fussy was sudden and unexpected. The three fireflies had been so bright that the change was almost painful. Nevertheless, she didn't hurt. The surrounding force was warm and soft. The new circumstance came complete with a new set of mixed aromas. Her moth was still below her, reposed in a frozen state of inactivity. For that split second all was still. Fussy thought they were so close and if only this restriction would go away. What seemed like the response to her wish, the surrounding, warm confinement, blossomed like a flower, allowing her to perceive the source of her new predicament.

She sat, with her uninjured mount, in the palm of the baseball glove-like hand of Redd Peppers. He smiled and extended an arm to accentuate his new offer of freedom.

"I'm so sorry. I acted by impulse. We have been

waiting for your return, and I've looked at a thousand fireflies and moths."

"I was so excited when you came up out of the field and past this tree, I just naturally grabbed you, and didn't want to lose you."

"That is all right. Fidget is just behind me with Jump, still in the darkness."

"What! You have found him? Hurrah!" Redd could hardly contain himself with shouting and jumping up and down with joy. Redd reached into the darkness as Fidget zipped by. He allowed Fidget to continue unencumbered as an exhausted boy with outstretched arms greeted Redd's huge teddy bear embrace.

"Hello there! Welcome home laddie," he said as he picked up the tired and bedraggled youth. He hugged him repeatedly as they twirled in little circles going up the lawn to the house.

"He's found. Jump is home," Redd shouted as he neared the house and saw two surprised ladies coming towards him with out stretched motherly arms.

Mater caught him in an exchange with Redd. Then, all of them moved towards the lighted house and its beckoning open kitchen door.

The Smidgens, receiving the good news of Jump's return. Were doing all kinds of acrobatics around the group and only slowed down when all were inside. Tears were flowing, and blubbering noises made by each, as hands tried to touch the lad to confirm his return.

Bakka entered the scene and fell right into the chorus of happy and relieved persons. Jump could scarcely take it all in. One time he would smile, and the next moment the hurt and wounds of a year lost away flooded through his countenance. Tears flowed like warm but salty honey.

Words poured from feminine voices. "A warm bath." "Clean clothes." "Milk and cookies." "A good nights rest." "Everything is going to be all right now." "You're are safe with us now."

All the right words soon acted like a tranquilizer. Jump's eyes were heavy, and he was half-asleep on his feet. Golly carried him upstairs at the direction of Mater and with motherly ministrations he was back in his own bed, fast asleep. Mater stayed in his room and just watched Jump with loving eyes redeemed from the pits of despair.

Golly returned to the kitchen. There was much to discuss even as the sun began to send first light to the world of the Smidgens.

The two Bright Ones had given their moths leave, and were in the kitchen, savoring the goodness of Bakka's talents. They talked for a long time and agreed that Golly had decided that all the Smidgens should return to the outdoors and to their natural lifestyle.

One vehicle with Empire and the chief detective came back and were thrilled and pleased that Jump had found his way home.

Mater had returned to the first floor when the sound of the vehicles approached. The detective thought it a mystery how a little boy could find his way home so far away in the dark.

"It is unusual for a boy to be able to know that his home is in a certain direction, and a certain distance after being blindfolded and kidnapped."

The detective continued, "we caught up with the

Grufflys just as they were trying to leave. They both soon confessed to all and blamed it all on the Pinching's gang and even implicated old Mr. Snooty. One of my men went down a little way from the house and caught their old dog. He was all cut up and trying to walk around a bush. He was very confused. I think he must have had a canine nervous breakdown. He had cuts and scratches all over his body.

Well it seems as though we have it all wrapped up. Thanks to the household, here at Rustic Realm we are able to close this case and close down a significant drug ring. We want to thank all of you for your help and participation." The detective closed with a salute and headed for the door.

His men and the four wheelers were shortly out of sight, and the room again was quiet.

"Is it all right to go up and look at our boy," said Empire?

" Mater said, "let's both go up and watch Jump grow,"

As they slowly ascended the stairs, arm in arm, Golly went back to the kitchen with Bakka.

The Smidgens were waiting out of sight as usual when the officers had returned.

"We are going up, join our clan, and get some rest. We can hardly keep our eyes open," the two Bright Ones said to no one in particular. Off they went via their secret ways and means.

"Oh, look, here comes our old errant cat," Bakka pointed through the door and down the lawn.

Slowly approaching the back door was Peyton. He looked like last years wet laundry. Limping and with hair missing in some places he held his head to one side to protect a swollen eye from the light from the approaching new day.

"Now what to you suppose he has been into? Off on one of his forays in the weeds I guess. Scaring little birds and chasing mice for the thrill of it. I don't know what Jump see's in him. At least he will be happy to know Jump has been found and is home. How are we going to tell him?" Bakka finished her scolding by putting out fresh milk for Peyton.

"I think he knows a lot more that we give him credit for," said Golly. "I think I'll go up and see whether the Uppitys' need anything before I turn in. What a day this has been. It just goes to show that a little flight can turn into something big. We need to remember that even small things can be so important as well as small people. Bakka, why don't you give that old black cat a second portion of milk and some cat food so that he can recuperate more quickly?"